Into the Black

Book Four

Jana` Chantel

About Right Media Group | Detroit, MI | 2025

About Right Media Group, LLC.
http://www.aboutrightmedia.com

Into the Black
Copyright © 2025 Jana` Chantel

Library of Congress Cataloging-in-Publication Data
Names: Chantel, Jana`, 1988—author.
Title: Fighting Red/ Jana` Chantel
Description: Detroit: About Right Media Group, LLc. 2025. | Series: Into the Black; 4
Identifiers: LCCN 2025919859 (print) |
(ebook) | ISBN 978-1-7330788-8-7 (hardcover) | ISBN 978-1-7330788-9-4 (paperback)
Subjects: | BISAC: FICTION/ Science Fiction/Apocalyptic & Post-Apocalyptic. | FICTION/ Science Fiction/ Action & Adventure. | FICTION/African American/General.
Classification: LCC 2025919859 (print)
LC record available at https://lccn.loc.gov/2025919859

Cover design by Moe Balinger and Fred Evans
Book Design by Jana` Evans

Printed in the United States of America
10   9   8   7   6   5   4

~*New York*~

Sunday

As she took cover behind a nearby tree, it seemed she would never catch her breath. She heard multiple footsteps running away. This was what Sunday hated: the chase. It always frightened her. The state of the world she lived in never frightened her... until moments like this, when people showed her how scary this world could be. Sunday closed her eyes and tried to listen. It sounded like her pursuers had run off in the opposite direction. She counted to three and then ran from behind her hiding place.

"There!" someone shouted. "There she is!"

"Shit! Grab her!"

Sunday fought back a scream as two grown men chased after her. At that moment, she became aware of how young she was. In reality, she shouldn't be out here alone. But she lost her group so long ago. And strangers could be terrifying—case in point, her current pursuers.

They couldn't catch her. If captured, she'd be sold off, and Sunday simply couldn't live with that fate.

"Get back here, you little shit!"

Sunday couldn't help but snort in response. Did this guy really think she would stop and let herself be caught? Seriously, how stupid was he? Sunday broke into a full sprint once she crossed the forest's tree line. She could hear the men behind her gasping to keep up.

A warehouse appeared ahead. Sunday headed toward the alley beside it, confident she could lose them there. The landscape was familiar terrain. Sunday had lived in this area for as long as she could remember, and no one knew it better than she did. She quickly glanced back to see how close the men were; they were out of sight. Satisfaction flashed on her face. Then, she abruptly came to a skidding halt.

There were three people at the end of the alley: two large, muscular men and a woman with a threatening look. The woman was helping one of the men to their feet. All three briefly smiled at each other and exchanged a few words. They hadn't noticed her yet. Sunday wasn't sure what she should do.

Were they with the guys who were chasing her? Were they planning to do something to her if they saw her? Should she run to another alley? Sunday was frozen.

Then, one of the men saw her. "Well, hello there."

"Don't talk to her," the woman snapped.

Sunday was confused. It seemed the woman didn't like this man. The woman slowly moved a few steps toward her. Sunday instinctively stepped back. The woman paused.

"Hey!" one of her pursuers yelled. They had finally tracked her down.

Sunday didn't think. She immediately ran past the woman toward the end of the alley. But the woman grabbed her arm before she got too far.

"You know them?"

Sunday shook her head. "They're trying to take me."

"Where?" the other man demanded. Although he was big, he didn't seem as intimidating as the other one. He appeared more friendly.

"To a place no girl or woman wants to be," Sunday never realized how childish her voice sounded until now. It was these people. They seemed so big and intimidating.

The woman frowned and nodded.

"Release her!" one of her pursuers shouted.

"You want her?" The woman turned around to face them, drawing two knives from her thigh strap. "Come get her."

The pursuers chuckled. "Well, you're worth a lot too, lady."

The two men charged at the woman. Sunday stumbled backward but was caught by the friendlier man.

"Don't worry, she won't let them hurt you," he assured her.

"But what about her?" Sunday looked up at him. He smiled back and then nodded toward the fight.

Sunday looked around and was astonished and frightened at what she saw. The two men lay bloodied on the ground. She had seen enough dead bodies to understand what she was looking at. It was over before it even began.

Who was this woman?

"You ok?" the woman asked as she turned around, revealing a bloody face. It was clearly the men's blood.

Sunday nodded.

"Is there anyone else with you?"

"Just me," Sunday's voice sounded so meek. It had been just little ol' her, by herself this whole time.

The second man whistled as he strolled over to the dead bodies. He laughed while inspecting them. "I must say, my sweet Jade, I really love your handiwork."

The woman rolled her eyes at him.

"You're Jade?" Sunday couldn't hide the admiration in her voice. She immediately started to kick herself for not noticing earlier. But the situation, coupled with the idea that she might be standing in front of this woman, didn't seem likely.

Jade frowned and nodded.

Sunday felt like she had to explain her sudden excitement. She pulled the folded, wrinkled papers out of her back pocket, unfolded them, and handed them to Jade. Jade took them and looked at them for a moment. She looked back at Sunday in disbelief.

"You've kept these."

Sunday nodded. "For moments when I need to be brave, I take out those posters and pretend to be strong, just like you."

Sunday couldn't understand the look Jade was giving her, but she recognized a look of sadness at one point. Jade finally handed back her posters.

"Alright," Jade sighed. "Come with us."

"Are you leaving New York?" Sunday panicked a little. She's never been out of New York.

"I need to get back to my sister," Jade paused. "Will you please help me?"

Sunday was stunned. Jade was asking her for help. *Jade*—the woman's wanted poster she'd been staring at every day. And now, she was standing right before her—Sunday's hero. Sunday took a deep breath. She looked at Jade's face.

Be brave.

"Of course, I'll help you."

Jade smiled and looked at the two men she was with, then nodded. She started to walk out of the alley, and Sunday quickly followed. As she watched Jade walk ahead of her, Sunday couldn't help but feel like she was walking with her into a fight.

~1~

Helena

If she hadn't heard the faint whistle in the air, Helena might have thought an earthquake was shaking the building. But no. This wasn't a natural disaster; it was an attack. The Radicals had struck HQ, and Jade and Razor had been captured. Helena was at a loss on how to respond. An overwhelming rage consumed her, and she needed to release it.

Tatianna and Keeper raced down the steps behind her. As the building shuddered for the umpteenth time, Helena's hand instinctively went to her belly. This had become a habit. She needed to ensure the little bean inside her was okay. Taking a deep breath, she continued to command central. As she neared the floor, she silently prayed that the protective corset Keeper had made for her would keep her little bean safe.

As soon as the door to command central opened, chaos erupted. Helena was right: this was an attack by the Radicals. Black Coats members fought desperately for their lives. It didn't take long before some Radicals charged at her. She met them head-on.

"Helena!" Tatianna shouted as she intervened. "Just stay back!"

"Don't start babying me, Tati," Helena quickly stabbed a Radical who got too close to her. "I'm not sitting this one out."

Helena looked around, trying to take in as much as she could. Zara, Cole, and Jackson were in the middle of command central. Most of the Radicals were gathering toward them. Reagan, Clay, Yoko, and Danita were farther back, struggling to reach them. Helena looked to see if Liam, the leader of the Radicals, was there. She couldn't spot him amid all the chaos.

"Get to Cole," Helena directed Tatianna and Keeper. The three of them slowly moved toward the leader of the Black Coats. "What's the plan?"

"We need to evacuate," Zara grunted as she fought off an attacker. "Quickly!"

"We have to take one of them alive," Helena dodged a knife thrown her way. "I need information on Jade and Razor's whereabouts."

"I know where they are," Zara stated.

"I'm sure they've already been moved by now," Tatianna countered. "It's only been a few hours."

Cole swiftly took out an attacker. "I believe she's right, Zara. I doubt they'd keep them in the same spot for long. We need to get information out of someone."

Helena fought to hold back the panic threatening to take over. She desperately needed to find out where her sister and husband were being held. She needed them now more than ever. Tears almost escaped her eyes. She cried out as she charged at two Radicals approaching her.

Rage consumed her. The thought of never seeing the two people she loved most again drove her into a feeling she couldn't explain. All Helena wanted in that moment was to kill—to hurt others and make them feel the fear and panic she was experiencing. This was the feeling that overtook her as she killed Radical member after Radical member. Then she heard Jackson yell.

"Down!" he shouted as he tackled her to the ground—shielding her.

A fiery blast followed instantly. Helena covered her ears, but it was no use. The explosion was deafening. There was a brief silence before screams and cries erupted into the air. Helena's heart pounded with worry. Jackson shifted for a moment, then slowly stood up. He reached out his hand to help Helena to her feet.

Fear ran through her as Helena surveyed the scene. It was devastating. There were numerous dead bodies scattered around. Helena didn't realize that so many of them were fighting in the room. Anxiety overwhelmed her as she searched for familiar faces in the crowd.

Helena began to move before Jackson stopped her. "Are you okay?" His hand immediately went to her stomach.

Helena quickly swatted it away. It was a reflex. "Sorry," she grumbled. "I'm good."

Jackson nodded.

Tears streamed down Helena's face as she looked around the burning room. "Tati!" she yelled. It seemed like she should have heard something from them by now. "Tati!"

"Fuck," Jackson whispered as he looked around. He paused for a moment, bent down, and gathered their weapons that weren't far away. "We should move."

Helena followed him through the rubble. "Tati! Keeper!"

"Aaahh!"

"My arm!"

"Help! Please, help!"

Tears flowed harder down Helena's face. The room's atmosphere was grim. All she could see were fallen Black Coats members. Listening to the pain and suffering of the surviving members was too much.

"Tati!! Keeper!!" Why weren't they responding? She couldn't bear the thought of them being dead, too.

Jackson took Helena's hand and helped her over a large piece of rubble. "We have to keep moving," his voice sounded distant and emotionless. Wasn't he worried, too? About the others? About his dad?

"Keeper! Tati!" Helena waited for a response. When she still didn't hear anything, she stopped walking. She hunched over, feeling like she couldn't breathe. "I can't do this," she whispered.

"Helena, we need to keep moving," Jackson said, placing a hand on her back. "We're almost out."

Helena looked up at him in disbelief. "You're not worried?"

Jackson shrugged. "I only care about you."

Helena frowned at him. What the hell was he saying? Why did he only care about her?

Jackson studied her face carefully. He sighed and shook his head. "I owe it to Jade to keep you safe. Especially now."

Helena was speechless. Jackson took her hand again and led them toward an exit. As they saw the outside, Helena could hear more fighting going on.

"Helena!"

"Tati?" Helena's heart raced. "Tati!"

"Helena!"

It sounded like the voice was coming from the exit they were heading toward. Jackson sped up and quickly cleared the remaining rubble blocking their way out, then helped Helena out through the makeshift exit.

As soon as she stepped outside, Helena was wrapped in someone's arms. She immediately recognized it as Tatianna's. Helena's body grew weak in her grip.

"Tati," she cried. Tatianna kissed the top of her head.

"I'm ok."

"Keeper?" Helena asked as she was released from Tatianna's embrace.

Tatianna nodded toward where Keeper was. He and Cole were helping a couple of injured members. Zara was finishing off the last Radical member present. Helena felt relief instantly, but then dread quickly took over.

"The others? Where are they?" Helena looked around in a panic. "Oh my God, where's Clay?"

Although she was initially suspicious of him, Helena realized how important he was to her sister. He truly was helping her—at least in the best way he knew. Jade needed him. Helena understood that. And she had to make sure he was alive.

"We can't worry about them now," Jackson said. "We need to move."

"Why are you being so cold?!" Helena snapped. "They're our people!"

"Look around, Helena! There's nothing left here. We have to go!"

Before she could respond, gunshots rang out.

For the first time in her life, Helena blacked out with rage. When she finally regained consciousness, she was dragging a beaten, tied, and gagged Radical member. She passed by the remaining group—the captive's muffled screams echoing in the air. They all stared at her in shock. Helena glanced at her bloodstained hands. Her pants and shoes were also covered in blood. This was the first time she felt more like Jade.

"*Now* we move," she stated as she walked past Jackson.

~2~

Jade

The growl of Jade's stomach seemed to grow louder by the second. Razor glanced at her with a raised eyebrow. Bossman even chuckled.

"I believe we're all feeling like that, my love."

"I am *not* your *fucking* love!"

The girl, Sunday, looked over at her with a puzzled expression. Jade's annoyance at Bossman's presence hadn't gone unnoticed by the girl. She seemed very perceptive for someone so young. Jade couldn't determine her age. She had been trying to figure it out over the last few days—since Jade insisted that she travel with them. Razor told Jade to ask the girl her age, but Jade felt like she had waited too long to ask.

If she had to guess, and Jade definitely was, Jade would have estimated the girl's age around eight. That possible knowledge caused Jade to feel a wave of anxiety.

"You did the right thing," Raina said as she appeared beside her.

They were currently in the backyard of an abandoned house. Their food search had been a failure, and they needed a break to regain some energy. It had been days since they last ate, and everyone was starting to feel the effects of hunger. Of course, Razor and Bossman were handling it better than she was. But Jade wasn't sure if it was the presence of the little girl that made her more on edge or the lack of food.

"I hope so," Jade grumbled. She saw Sunday standing close to Bossman. "Get away from him."

"Jade," Razor sighed. He had definitely noticed how on edge she was.

"I said, move away from him," Jade said, standing up from the back porch where she was sitting.

Sunday looked between Jade and Razor. After a few seconds, she moved a few feet away from Bossman.

"Is this really necessary?" Bossman asked.

"He's a child killer," Jade said to Sunday. A flicker of fear flashed across Sunday's face. "Do you know who he is?"

Sunday nodded. "The creator of the DC task force," she paused and looked uncomfortable for a second. "But he's traveling with you, so I thought he was ok."

Bossman laughed at that.

"Let's move out," Razor said, rising from the crate he was resting on. "We need to find food."

Jade frowned as Bossman followed Razor out of the backyard. Sunday shifted nervously on her feet, uncertain of what to do. Jade looked at her, her heart pounding as she watched Sunday's skinny, petite frame. She appeared so innocent and adorable. Her curly hair was styled in two French braids pulled to the back. Jade watched her every morning as she took her hair out of the braids, detangled it, and then re-braided it into French braids.

"I prefer them neat," Sunday explained to her when she caught Jade watching her.

Her ripped jeans, faded T-shirt, and combat boots gave her an appearance that seemed older and tougher. But Jade knew the truth. Sunday was just a scared little girl trying to get through each day in this frightening world.

"She needs you," Raina encouraged. "You got this, Jade."

Jade looked at Sunday. Sunday was still waiting for instructions from Jade.

"Let's go," Jade said as she started to walk out of the backyard. "Just keep your distance from him."

"I didn't mean to get so close," Sunday said as she followed Jade out of the backyard.

Razor and Bossman were walking in the middle of the street. Jade looked around, feeling a little leery. They hadn't come across anyone in a while, which was strange. She felt like they should've encountered someone by now, like the guys who were chasing after Sunday, but they hadn't seen anyone like that. It looked like no man's land, making Jade very skeptical.

"Let's try here," Razor suggested, pointing to a building that looked like it had once been a bodega.

Sunday sighed. "You won't find anything in there," Razor turned to glare at her. Sunday rolled her eyes. "I'm telling you, you won't find anything around here."

"We're not having this argument again," Jade said. They have been arguing for days now over getting food.

"Then we're all gonna starve," Sunday stopped walking.

Bossman chuckled but didn't say a word.

"We're not going along with your idiotic plan, so just drop it," annoyance filled Razor's voice.

"It's not idiotic!" Sunday glared at him. "I do it all the time, and I can keep myself fed! You're the one being a scared piece of shit and won't do it!"

At this, Bossman burst out laughing.

"Watch your mouth!" Razor stomped over toward her.

Sunday looked up at him, fists clenched, but Jade could see them trembling. "I'm not afraid of you."

Jade let out a sigh. "Enough."

"I'm not stupid," Sunday turned toward her—ignoring Razor's looming presence behind her. "It's the only way to get food around here. Every place around here has been picked clean."

"You want us to rob the group of men who've been hunting you down," Razor stated with anger.

"Not rob, steal," Sunday corrected. "Those assholes are too stupid to realize that anything's missing."

"Watch your mouth," Razor warned her again.

"But they are assholes!" Sunday sighed when Razor rolled his eyes at her. "What would you call a group of men who kidnapped girls and women and forced them to work in sex houses?"

"Limp-dickwads?" Jade shrugged.

Sunday laughed. "Oh, that's perfect! They're limp-dickwads."

Razor threw his hands up in frustration.

"What?" Jade laughed. "If you can't beat her..."

"It's fun when you join in," Sunday said, grabbing Razor's hand. All traces of anger vanished from her face. "Try it, Razor!"

"Fine, where do we find these assholes?" Razor asked, defeated.

"No! You have to come up with a new name."

Razor looked over at Jade for help. She just shrugged. Razor appeared a little frazzled as he looked down at Sunday. It seemed like she was having a weird effect on him, too. "Show us where we can find these shitlickers," Razor sighed.

Sunday laughed with joy as she led the way. Bossman tried to hide his laughter as he followed her. Razor closed his eyes and shook his head tiredly. Jade approached him and placed a comforting hand on his shoulder. She looked at him with sympathy.

"We couldn't leave her by herself.

"I know we did the right thing," he said, watching as Sunday marched down the street, Bossman shaking his head while following her. "She's just a little much sometimes."

Jade began following them. "At least she's a good distraction."

"More like a frightening glimpse of the future."

"I hate to break it to you," Jade chuckled. "It might be a little worse."

"Great," Razor sighed.

"I was just joking," Jade nudged his shoulder to make him smile. Razor didn't budge. "Look, we'll stock up on food, rest for the night, and then speed up our trip to Helena."

Razor let out a sigh of relief. "Sounds good."

Jade hurried up to catch Sunday. Bossman was getting too close for her comfort. She knew she couldn't keep the two of them apart forever, but it eased her anxiety. When she finally reached Sunday, Jade slowed down to match her pace. Sunday smiled when she saw Jade, and Jade returned the smile. They all stayed quiet as they followed Sunday into a wooded area.

Bossman glanced at Jade before clearing his throat. "Uh, little one,"

Sunday paused and turned to face him. "Do you have a plan here?"

Sunday glanced at Jade as if asking for permission to speak. Jade nodded. Sunday then gestured toward a trail to their left.

"This is one of the routes these limp-dickwads take," Sunday looked down the path. "I'm not sure where they get their supplies from, but they're always stocked with food and such."

"And how do you know about this path?" Bossman asked.

"Vivian scouted it out a long time ago," Sunday stated. "The gang and I used to hit it all the time."

"Vivian?" Jade asked.

"The gang?" Razor asked at the same time.

"Vivian was like a... crap, what's the word for it, like a foster mother?" Sunday looked at Jade with a frown. After a few seconds, she shrugged. "She was friends with my mother. Anyway, they're all dead now. But before that, we used to hit this path all the time. I haven't been here in a while, though."

Jade and Razor exchanged looks—silent questions passing between them.

"Do you have a weapon?" Bossman pressed on.

"No," Sunday frowned. "We're not fighting them."

Bossman pulled out a baton and a knife. "With the amount of supplies we'll need, I can assure you you'll need a weapon."

"It's better if we don't fight," Sunday looked at Jade with fear in her eyes.

"We might not have a choice in this matter," Jade said.

Sunday reluctantly took the weapons from Bossman. She pulled an empty knife holster out of her backpack and clipped it to her belt loop. She placed the knife inside. Sunday twirled the baton in her hand as she pressed her boot into the dirt.

"Are you familiar with fighting with that?" Jade pointed to the holstered knife.

Sunday nodded without glancing at any of them.

Bossman started walking down the trail. "Let's go, I'm starving."

"Um, what about the plan?" Jade asked.

"I am the plan."

"Shit," she mumbled, a sinking feeling settling in as they followed.

~3~

Clay

This had to be one of the worst moments of his life. Clay had to admit he'd experienced some doozies before, but nothing seemed to compare to this—or so it seemed. The news just came in that the Radicals have captured Jade and Razor. As Clay was preparing to go out and rescue them, the Radicals launched a surprise attack, throwing another wrench into his already bad day.

It was easy to spot Reagan, Danita, and Yoko when the attack first began. The three women were usually always together. Clay tried to come up with a plan to find Helena as they fought in command central. He needed to ensure she was okay. But as time went on, they backed themselves further into a corner at the back of command central.

For a brief moment, he thought luck was finally on his side when Helena, Keeper, and Tatianna entered command central. But alas, he was once again deceived when another explosion occurred. Reagan knocked him to the ground just in time. It felt like Clay was having an out-of-body experience. How many things could go wrong in such a short amount of time?

Right now, the answer was everything.

Once the ringing in his ears finally subsided, the screams started. It was chaos. It seemed like everyone in the room was seriously hurt or dead—Radicals included.

"Reagan," Clay gasped as he tried to assess his injuries. "Talk to me."

"I'm alive," she gritted out. She was in pain. "I think my wrist might be broken, though."

Every part of Clay hurt right now, and it was hard to tell if he had any serious injuries. His left knee, though, was feeling a little wonky.

"Yoko. Danita," he didn't like the silence.

"I'll survive," Yoko coughed. "But Danita's bleeding from her head."

Clay tried to stand up but lost his balance. Something was definitely wrong with his knee. He was more successful on his second attempt. He hobbled over to Yoko and kneeled beside an unresponsive Danita.

"Shit," he mumbled. Blood was pooling from the back of her head. He was unsure of what to do. He never bothered to learn any kind of medical treatment. "Do we move her?"

"I don't know," Yoko's voice was full of panic. Clay could tell she wished she knew a bit more about medical things, too.

"We can put her on this," Reagan winced as she pulled a makeshift gurney over to them. "You two will have to lift her."

Clay looked at her injured wrist. It was clear she was in pain. They had to get out of the building quickly and find the others. Hopefully, the Doc made it out alive. Clay awkwardly got to his feet, and he and Yoko managed to get Danita onto the gurney.

Yoko looked at his left knee with concern. "Are you good on that knee?" Besides a few cuts and bruises, she seemed perfectly fine.

"I'll be ok," he assured her.

Yoko bore most of the weight as Clay adjusted to his good leg. Once he was steady, they carefully followed Reagan as she looked for an escape route.

"I think I see a way out up here," Reagan said as she led the way.

Clay winced as he landed wrong on his injured knee. "How far up?"

"Not that far."

Clay shifted his weight onto his good leg. How did they end up in this mess? They couldn't catch a break. The Radicals had been relentless, taking hits and suffering losses. They hardly trusted anyone in their group and kept looking over their shoulders. When would all of this end? At this point, Clay just wanted a moment of peace to clear his mind.

Despite everything, he still didn't regret stepping in to save debtors from the DC. He would never regret that. However, he did regret getting Reagan involved. Since they were little kids, they had always been close. He was just two years older than her, but they did everything together. Reagan was never an annoying little sister. Even when she thought some of his actions were wrong, she was always there—silently supporting him. Clay honestly didn't know what he'd do without her.

"Here," Reagan turned to face him. There was a look of worry. "You're going to have to climb."

She was right. Clay could see the huge piece of rubble blocking the exit. The only way out was to climb over it. It wasn't very steep, but enough to make his injured knee ache just by looking at it. Not to mention, he didn't know how they would get Danita out of there.

"I'll go first," Reagan suggested. "Maybe there'll be someone nearby who can help us out. Stay put."

Clay didn't like the idea of splitting up, but there really wasn't any other choice. They needed help. It was best to evacuate the building quickly. So Clay watched Reagan climb over the rubble and out of the building to get help. He was amazed she could do it despite her broken wrist. Sometimes, he was amazed by how strong and determined his sister was. It was easy for him to get used to that. And when he met Jade and the others, it became even easier not to acknowledge his sister's strength.

"Maybe we should put her down," Yoko suggested. From the tone of her voice, Clay could tell that Danita's weight was getting to her.

Clay nodded, and they gently laid Danita on the floor. It was at that moment that he took in his surroundings. Up until then, he had purposefully distracted himself. He didn't want to see the gore left behind by the fight. There had been so much of it lately that it was starting to affect him. How much gore and violence can one person handle? Clay was sure he had gone beyond the normal limit.

Although he chose not to look, the sound of the aftermath still reached his ears. People were groaning and begging for help. Clay shut his eyes and tried to block it out. His breathing quickened, and his chest felt tight. What was happening? He'd never experienced anything like this before. He needed to get out of there.

"Clay? Yoko?" Keeper's voice echoed from the other side of the rubble.

"We're here," Clay managed to say.

Keeper, Tatianna, and Jackson made their way over the large rubble. Clay was relieved to see them. Jackson helped Yoko with Danita while Keeper and Tatianna assisted Clay in climbing out. Once outside, it took a moment for Clay's eyes to adjust. He saw Reagan getting her wrist looked at by Cole. Zara and other Black Coats' members were keeping watch, and Helena had a beaten-up Radical tied up and gagged.

For a brief moment, Clay's heart stopped. The look on Helena's face told him that the violence and gore weren't about to end anytime soon.

~4~

Jade

The stiflingly warm breeze hit Jade's face as she crouched behind a tree. She readjusted into a more comfortable position. There was no clear indication of how long they'd been waiting for someone to appear on the trail, but Jade would estimate about an hour. According to Sunday, the "snatchers" (as she called them) frequent this trail all the time. Apparently, it's a direct route to their camp. The Snatchers would load up on supplies at their camp and then go on their way.

Bossman hung out on the trail as bait. The Snatchers were always cautious around new faces. Plus, they were sure the men would recognize Bossman. That's what made him the ideal bait. When the men tried to attack Bossman, Jade and Razor would jump out and ambush them. Sunday was to stay hidden during it all. Jade wasn't risking anything happening to her. Even though she had only known her for a few days, Jade couldn't bear the thought of harm coming to the girl.

"She's a lot tougher than you think," Raina assured as she appeared beside Jade.

"Still not willing to risk it," Jade looked over at Sunday's hiding spot. She was well tucked in among some overgrown bushes and shrubbery. If Jade hadn't seen her take cover there, she would never have known where Sunday was hiding. Jade sighed as she thought about how often Sunday had done this alone. How had she survived this long?

A shiver ran down Jade's spine as she thought about what Sunday must have done to stay alive.

"It's probably the same things you would've wanted me to do," Raina stated, reading Jade's mind.

Jade looked at the knife resting in her hand. Not long ago, she had thought that way. But now that she's around another child, she couldn't bring herself to do it. She wanted Sunday to stay just that—a child. But Jade feared she was a little too late.

"Yeah," Jade sighed. "I'm not so sure about that anymore."

Raina smiled. "I see you no longer want to taint the children of this world."

"No," Jade glanced back at the bushes and shrubbery. "I'm afraid this world has already done that."

Raina nodded silently, her face showing sadness.

Jade slowly peeked around the tree to see Bossman standing in the middle of the trail, digging his boot into the dirt. What she wouldn't give to drive her knife into his black heart right now, but she had to play nice. If she didn't, they'd never get back to Helena. Not quickly, anyway.

This was taking forever. How long did they have to wait before someone came down the trail? Jade quietly stretched and then stood. She was about to suggest they try something else when she heard multiple footsteps in the distance, followed by loud talking and laughter. She crouched back down in her hiding spot.

After a few seconds, she peeked out from behind the tree and saw that Bossman was casually leaning against one. Jade rolled her eyes. Of course, he was nonchalant about this situation. Was he serious about anything? Besides torturing and killing people?

The chatter grew louder, and Bossman yawned in response. Jade couldn't understand everything being said, but it seemed the group was swapping war stories. Jade was immediately annoyed. This looked like a group of people who didn't have a care in the world. She was sure they weren't debtors. Debtors didn't walk and laugh like this group did. And it didn't go unnoticed that the group was all men... *figures.*

"Whoa!" one of the men shouted. "What the hell are you doing here?"

"I heard this was the only way I could get some food around here," Bossman said.

"Do you know how much we can get for you?"

"The former asshole in charge of the DC," another man said in disgust. "My friends died because of you."

"Then I'm sure you'll be happy to join them."

The next moment, Jade heard scuffling. *Shit. Shit. Shit.* This was not the plan! He was supposed to confirm they had food first. Jade looked around, trying to recall where Razor was hiding. What should they do now? Should they step in? How many men were there? They never even checked that! This is what happens when you let a psychopath make a plan.

"Take him down!" a man shouted. More grunts and fighting were heard.

Jade heard Razor yell, and she reluctantly jumped out of her hiding spot. Everything had fallen apart so quickly. If these men weren't carrying food after all of this, Jade was sure she'd kill Bossman.

It was hard to tell how many men were present. Two were on Razor. Three were fighting Bossman. And another three were standing around, but Jade couldn't tell if more were coming.

"Oh, hell yeah!" another man shouted with glee when he saw Jade. She wasn't sure what was running through his mind, but she knew it wasn't good.

She didn't confront him directly. Instead, Jade waited for him to come closer. She pulled out another knife from her thigh strap. When he was near, she dodged his attack and quickly slit his throat. She then threw her second knife at the second man charging at her. He paused mid-attack as the knife hit him in the chest. His eyes widened as he slowly sank to his knees.

Razor was finished with the men he was fighting and moved on to the last one. Jade started walking toward the bags that the men had dropped, but a knife was hurled at her before she could get close. She barely dodged it in time. The blade grazed her cheek just above her combat mask. *Great.* More men were coming to join the fight. It seemed to be about five men.

Jade swiftly grabbed the knife that was thrown at her. She never missed an opportunity to expand her collection.

"Nice," Bossman said as he looked at the men approaching. Blood was on his face. "More supplies."

Jade rolled her eyes as she stood. "We don't even know if they have anything useful."

Bossman shrugged. "Only one way to find out," he charged at them with an enraged look in his eyes.

After a few seconds, Razor followed. Jade sighed as she lingered. The goal was not to overexert herself. Her attackers would come for her, and she did not doubt that. Still, she threw a knife as one man approached, but he dodged at the last second, and it landed in his shoulder. *Dammit.* Even after the hit, he kept moving quickly. Before she realized it, his arms were around her waist, and he was tackling her to the ground.

Jade struggled to free her arms. The guy moved awkwardly as he tried to pin her down with his good arm. Jade bit his arm. The man screamed as he loosened his grip and took a step back. Jade took that opportunity to wiggle an arm free and punched the knife deeper into the guy's shoulder. He grunted and punched Jade in the face, but the punch was weak. She swiftly snatched the knife from his shoulder and jabbed it into his gut. Blood dripped on her hands as the man's face twisted in pain. Jade shoved him away and got up.

Jade lost sight of Razor, Bossman, and the other men. But she saw Sunday sneaking around, gathering up the bags. Sunday was placing them in her hiding spot. Jade went to collect the bags that were near her. It was silent for a minute. Jade focused on picking up as many bags as she could, but after a while, the silence started to bother her. She began walking toward Sunday with the remaining bags when someone's arm wrapped around her neck.

Shit!

How out of it was she? Jade didn't even hear anyone walk up. Who were these people?

"Jade!" Sunday screamed. Another man rushed over and grabbed Sunday into his arms.

Jade yelled as she fought to escape the chokehold. Sunday thrashed wildly in her attacker's grip, trying to free herself. Jade struggled to breathe. *No. No. No.* This couldn't be real. Not again! It all felt like déjà vu. Sunday's nose was scrunched up as she fought to break free from her attacker. The scene brought to mind Raina's face when she tried to escape from that DC officer.

Not again. Not again. Not again.

Jade screamed again as she bent down and threw her attacker over her shoulder—her combat nebulizer coming loose in the process.

"Jade!" Sunday screamed in terror. "Help!"

Jade pulled out a knife and stabbed her attacker in the chest. She looked up to see the other guy walking away with Sunday.

"Don't let him take me!"

"Sunday!" Jade rushed to chase after them, but the guy she just stabbed grabbed her foot and made her trip. Jade hit the ground hard on her face. She could feel her lip bleeding. She looked back to see the guy smirking as the life slowly drained from his eyes. Jade wriggled free from his grip and got back on her feet.

The other guy started to run, putting more distance between himself and Jade. Panic began to take hold of Jade. She thought she was going to lose her. Another child was about to die on her watch. Sunday was going to suffer because Jade failed. It felt like her feet couldn't move fast enough. Every stick, branch, and rock seemed to appear in her path. She tripped and stumbled as she desperately tried to catch up. There was no way she could save her.

"Raina!" Jade exclaimed, then she realized her slip of the tongue. "Sunday!"

"Jade!" Sunday's scream sounded farther away.

"Sunday!" Tears blurred Jade's vision, but she kept running. No matter how slow it seemed she was moving, Jade didn't dare stop. If she did, she'd definitely lose Sunday for good.

Then, Sunday screamed at the top of her lungs. A man's scream followed, sounding like he was in pain. Jade ran faster and finally caught sight of them. Sunday was on the ground with the guy, leaning over him. She screamed again, raising her knife and stabbing the guy once more. The man yelled. Sunday repeated the process—again, and again, and again. The man no longer yelled.

Jade sprinted to her and quickly wrapped Sunday in her arms—holding her tightly. Sunday was stiff as she clutched the knife in her bloody hands.

"It's ok," Jade whispered. "It's all over."

Sunday stayed frozen, gazing at the man she had just killed.

"I'm so sorry," Jade cried as she kissed Sunday's forehead. "I'm sorry I couldn't get to you sooner."

Jade couldn't tell how long they sat there—Sunday wrapped in her arms. The dead body was not even an inch away from them. It was unbelievable. Sunday managed to save herself. Jade wasn't sure if she should be proud or sad about that. But Sunday was still here. She could still see another day, and for that, Jade was grateful.

"Jade," panic filled Razor's voice as he approached them. Jade was so relieved that Sunday wasn't taken; she had forgotten all about him and Bossman. She noticed that he had her combat nebulizer in his hand. He kneeled beside her. "Are you ok?"

"They almost took her," she whispered. Sunday was still frozen in her arms.

Razor looked at Sunday with concern, his gaze fixed on her hands. "Did she..."

"She saved herself," Jade finished.

Bossman stepped in front of them. He carefully took the knife from Sunday's grasp. He handed her a damp cloth. "Clean your hands, little one. You did well."

Sunday looked over at Jade—the first movement she'd made since everything happened. Her eyes sought permission. Jade nodded. Sunday slowly wiped her hands—blood barely coming off. Razor handed Jade her combat nebulizer as he examined her. His glance lingered on the cut on her cheek.

"Are they dead?" Jade asked. She felt a strong urge to hunt down everyone in this group and make them suffer. They deserved to be hurt.

"Everyone who came this way," Bossman stated.

"The bags?" Razor asked. "We only saw a few of them on the ground."

"The rest are hidden," Sunday said. Her voice was raspy from all the screaming. "I put them in the bushes where I was hiding."

Razor nodded.

Bossman looked around and sighed. "Let's get out of here," he said, looking down at Jade. "If anyone else comes back, I'm afraid you two won't be any fun."

Jade didn't even feel like rolling her eyes at him. She released Sunday from her hold and slowly stood up. Sunday followed. She looked at the dead man—his shirt covered in blood from all the stab wounds.

Jade gently grabbed Sunday's chin and guided her to look at Jade. "You did the right thing," Jade had to make sure Sunday didn't feel guilty. "It was either you or him...choose you every time."

Sunday nodded and looked back at the dead man. After a few seconds, she nodded again.

**

They settled down for the night in an abandoned store far from the Snatchers' trail. It was a quiet journey. Jade kept replaying how helpless she felt when Sunday was almost taken away from her. That would never happen again. She wouldn't let her fear cripple her like that again. Sunday was silent for a different reason. Jade could tell she was thinking about the man she killed. She remembered what that felt like. Now, Jade could barely remember any of their faces—and she no longer cared to.

Razor and Bossman were unusually quiet as well. Jade didn't understand why. Once they settled into the store, they went over the supplies they had taken. It was a significant haul. They had plenty of food, weapons, and supplies to last a while, at least until they reached Helena and the others. They organized the supplies into four bags, one for each of them to carry. After that, they ate dinner in silence. Bossman hummed now and then, which irritated Jade. But everything he did irritated her.

After they ate, Jade cleaned herself up as best she could and even helped clean the blood off Sunday's hands. Afterwards, she found a spot to sleep in the back of the store, with Sunday beside her.

"I'll take the first watch," Razor stated. "We leave at first light."

Jade nodded as she embraced Sunday. Sunday snuggled into Jade's chest. After a few minutes, Jade could hear the deep breaths of her sleeping. Jade quickly followed suit.

Then, she was awakened by a stir. Her arms were empty. Sunday! Where was Sunday? Jade looked around frantically. Sunday was nowhere in sight. Jade sprang to her feet. Maybe she went out front. Jade hurried to the front room. Bossman sat in the corner with a hard-to-read expression on his face. Jade followed his gaze. Sunday was in Razor's arms, shaking and crying. Razor gently rocked her and kissed the top of her head.

"You're safe," he whispered. "You're safe."

The scene broke her heart. There was no need for Jade to save the children of this world. The children were already adapting to it.

~5~

Razor

Never in his life did Razor think he'd become a father… not when the world was normal, and definitely not when it ended. He never believed it was possible. Even with Raina and Levi, they never quite felt like his own… no matter how much he wished it to be. But something was different about Sunday. He wasn't sure if it was her personality or the fact that she'd managed to survive all this time on her own. Still, he couldn't stop his heart from pounding in his chest when she sprinted out of the back room, frightened by a nightmare, and threw herself into his arms for comfort. There were only two people in this world who could provoke that kind of reaction from him—the Willer sisters. And now, it seemed

Sunday was one of them.

"Stop fidgeting, Jade!" Sunday snapped.

"Then be gentle!" Jade snapped back.

Nick chuckled as Razor smiled and shook his head. Looking at her now, you'd never guess that she had spent most of the night trembling and crying in his arms. Sunday kept whispering that she was a murderer. It broke Razor's heart. He spent the rest of the night comforting her.

Now, it seemed like roles were reversed as Jade sat between Sunday's legs while Sunday frowned at the mess of Jade's hair.

"Seriously, how old are you?" Sunday fussed. "I'm nine and can keep my hair looking decent."

Jade sighed in frustration. "I have other things on my mind besides hair."

"Then cut it."

"Ugh, you sound like my sister."

Nick cleared his throat. "Um, how much longer, ladies?"

"I'll need some time," Sunday said. "I have a lot to work on."

"Ow!"

"Sorry!"

Nick laughed as he walked toward the front door. He glanced at Razor. "Should we do a quick perimeter check then?"

Razor nodded. "We should have been on the road already."

Nick glanced at Sunday and Jade, then back at him. "You try telling the little one that."

"Pass," Razor said, opening the door. Sunday was determined to do Jade's hair, and Razor didn't have the energy to argue with her. It was best to let her win this battle.

Nick laughed as he walked out. Razor followed. It was eerily quiet outside. Razor didn't understand it. Why was this area no man's land?

Was it because of the snatchers? Were they causing that much chaos for the people around here? He also noticed there were barely any DC patrols around.

"Something's wrong," he stated.

"Chase is using the DCs to search for us," Nick responded. "Who cares about medical debtors anymore?"

Razor looked over at him with a raised eyebrow.

"Right now, Chase is only concerned with saving face," Nick continued.

"Do you regret it?" Razor asked.

"What are you referring to?" Nick asked, looking away. Razor knew Nick was pretending not to know. But he couldn't really blame him. If he'd done something like that, he'd act clueless, too.

"Killing the children," Razor stated. "Do you regret it?"

Nick stopped walking. "I'd be fucking heartless if I didn't."

Razor nodded and glanced around. "Let's get back inside."

"Yeah, there's no action out here," Nick said as he headed back to the front door of the store.

Razor took one last glance before following him. When they got back inside, Sunday had three French braids in Jade's hair and was working on another one. There was no telling how many braids she was trying to put in Jade's head. Jade's face was scrunched up as Sunday worked on the braid.

"Could you be any rougher?" Jade complained.

"Could your head be any more tender?!"

"We need to find a quick way back to Toronto," Razor interrupted their arguing.

"Yeah," Jade winced. "Walking isn't going to cut it."

"Oh, that's easy," Sunday stated. "We can just steal a DC truck."

Instead of saying no, Razor chose a different approach. "There are no

DCs around."

"Sure, there are," Sunday paused on the braid she was working on. "They're on Snatchers' Row."

"Snatchers' Row?" Razor wondered where she got these names.

Sunday nodded as she continued to braid Jade's hair. "That's the name of the street where the Snatchers bring all the women and children to...anyway, there's this lot where DCs can park their trucks while they're being 'entertained.' It's a great place to steal a truck."

"Absolutely not," Razor said.

"Let's do it," Nick quickly responded.

Jade winced again. "Seriously, how do you know about this?"

"Vivian and the gang," Sunday stated as if it was obvious.

"What other options do we have?" Jade asked, shrugging as she looked at Razor.

Razor's heart was pounding. Sunday and her plans were going to be the death of him.

**

"Stop pouting and come on, Razor," Sunday whispered as she led him down Snatchers' Row. They were currently crawling through a thicket of grass and weeds in a field right across the street from the row of houses.

This was a terrible idea, and Razor was trying to figure out how he got involved in it. Jade and Nick were acting as lookouts at each end of the block while he and Sunday went to the lot that held the DC trucks. He wanted Sunday to stay back, but Jade was insistent that she go with Razor instead.

"I can't afford to freeze up again," she admitted. "And there's no way in hell I'm letting her be alone with Bossman."

"It's more dangerous if she goes in with me," Razor pointed out.

"But you won't freeze up."

Razor sighed at that. Jade had a point. He wouldn't freeze up if Sunday were in danger. Still, he didn't want her there with him because it was too risky.

"Please, Razor," Jade begged. "Let's just finish this and get back to Helena."

Razor hesitantly agreed, and now here he was, following Sunday as she led him deeper into Snatchers' Row.

Like the rest of the country, Snatchers' Row was overrun with foliage and damage from natural disasters. But it still looked like the people in charge tried to keep up with the maintenance. Some weeds and other vegetation had been pulled or looked manicured. The houses had boarded-up windows and worn-looking doors. Even the roofs seemed patched up and repaired. Surprisingly, there were a lot of vehicles occupying the street. They were all broken down, of course, but Razor wondered why so many were there in the first place. He didn't dwell on the reason for it too long, and right now, they would provide excellent cover.

"Psst," he whispered before Sunday got too far away from him. He pointed to one of the abandoned cars when she turned around.

Sunday shook her head. "Those are traps," she nodded to the left. "This way will get us to the lot unseen."

Razor ignored all the questions forming in his mind and followed Sunday. He hated that she knew all the tricks and traps these people created. She was only nine years old. These were things she shouldn't even know about. But here she was, leading him to steal a car. Razor sighed. Focus on the plan.

Steal a truck.

Get back to Helena.

That was all he could worry about. He'd just have to be thankful that Sunday knew about this kind of thing.

It was eerily quiet on Snatchers' Row. Razor expected there to be much more activity than he had seen. Where were all the people? Where was the patrol? If they were snatching as many people as Sunday suggested, they should have heard all kinds of commotion.

"Something's wrong," Razor whispered as he paused.

"This is normal," Sunday assured. "Patrol looks out from the houses. And they keep their captives quiet. They don't want to draw too much attention to themselves."

Razor couldn't let the questions go. "How do you know all this?"

Sunday shrugged while continuing to crawl. "I helped someone escape."

Razor was about to ask a follow-up question when the grassy field transformed into gravel. Sunday paused at the edge of the field. She peeked through the tall grass, making sure the coast was clear.

"We gotta be quick," she warned.

"Let's go," Razor said as he got on his knees, preparing to run.

"Go," Sunday darted out of the field and ran toward a gate that was several feet away.

Razor was right behind her. She quickly slipped through an opening in the gate and held it open for him. Razor wiggled through. Sunday was right; there was a fleet of DC trucks parked in the lot. How long has this operation been around? It seemed like this was something he should've known about.

"Where's security?" he asked.

"There isn't one," Sunday looked around and ran to the first truck nearby. "They figured no one is brave enough to try to steal a truck." She reached into her backpack, pulled out a Slim Jim, and popped the lock to the truck. "Shit brains."

Sunday threw her backpack into the vehicle and got in the driver's seat.

"What are you doing?" Razor looked at her, confused. Surely, she didn't think she was driving.

"Keep a lookout, will ya," she said as she pulled out a knife and went for the steering wheel.

"Did you look for a key?"

Sunday shot him a look. "The officers are stupid, but they're not *that* stupid. I need to hotwire it."

Razor shook his head but kept a watchful eye on the situation. He couldn't shake his anxiety as he looked around the lot. It's not supposed to be this quiet. Someone had to be watching somewhere. Instinctively, he pulled out his machete—ready for an attack that would probably come. Sunday rummaged around some more, trying to start the truck.

"Come on, you nincomshit," she grumbled.

"I believe you mean nincompoop," Razor fought back a chuckle.

"I said what I said," Sunday kept at it. She continued to curse under her breath as she tried to figure out which wire would start the vehicle.

"I thought you'd done this before." Razor looked around again.

Sunday sighed. "Not all trucks are made equal."

Razor fought back a smile as he got under her skin. There was something about annoying her that felt like revenge. She was so bossy and insistent on doing specific things that it annoyed him. It seemed like she enjoyed messing with him. It was satisfying to turn the tables on her.

"Any day now," he urged.

"Let me focus," she hissed. She turned her attention back to the truck. "Come on, *work.*"

Razor paused at his retort when he realized something. Maybe she didn't know what she was doing. Maybe she was lying—trying to make herself seem more valuable to them. Maybe she was afraid they'd abandon her if she couldn't help them on their journey. Razor's heart sank as he turned toward her.

"Here, let me give you a hand."

"Got it!" she smiled triumphantly as the truck roared to life. Then her face turned to horror. "Razor, watch out!"

It all happened so quickly. Sunday moved forward, her arm thrusting past his face. Razor spun around to see a man right behind him with a bat mid-swing, frozen as a knife was embedded in his neck... Sunday's knife. She froze. Her slender frame trembled as she took in the scene.

"Shit," Razor pulled the knife out of the guy's neck, gently pushed Sunday into the passenger's seat, and got into the truck. He closed the driver's door as the guy dropped to the ground. Razor sped away, hoping Jade and Nick weren't in trouble.

"He..." Sunday whispered to herself. "He was gonna hurt you."

"It's ok," he said, handing Sunday her knife. "Clean and sheath it." He wasn't sure if that was the right choice, but she needed to protect herself. He couldn't allow another incident like Raina and Levi's to happen again.

Sunday followed Razor's instructions. When she finished, she looked at her hands. Tears streamed down her face as her hands shook.

"I just wanted to help," she cried.

Razor held her hand. "I know," he said, looking at her young face. How many people had she killed to be here today? "Thank you for having my back out there."

It didn't matter. He was thankful she came across them that day. Because of her, he could keep moving on to Helena.

And that was all that mattered.

~6~

Helena

As she sat on the crate, the captive swung back and forth by their ankles; Helena couldn't hold back the tears that fell. She hated doing this, but it had to be done. Usually, she left this kind of thing to Razor and even Jade. But not today. Today, it had to be done by her. Others had offered to do it for her. Tatianna, Clay, and Jackson all stepped forward to volunteer, but Helena declined them all. She had to do this herself. She needed to get the correct information to bring her family back.

The captive groaned. Helena looked at them. Blood was pooling down their face and spilling onto the floor. Helena cracked her knuckles. Interrogating people was very hard on her hands. She didn't understand how Razor could do it for so long.

Helena glanced at her bloodied, battered hands. "I'll ask this one last time," she paused, looking up at the captive. "Or I'm going to start breaking bones. Where are Razor and Jade being held?"

The captive spat on the floor. "Eat shit!"

"Ok," Helena smirked as she stood up. The captive twisted nervously as Helena gripped one of their fingers and snapped it back until she heard a satisfying crack. The captive screamed. Helena offered them no mercy. She broke two more fingers after that.

"Stop, stop, stop, stop!" the captive yelled and squirmed. "I'll tell you what you want to know."

Helena backed away, breathing heavily. This was all so exhausting that she felt like she could sleep for days afterward.

The captive cried and groaned in pain as they tried to collect themselves. "Please understand; I don't know if the plans have changed."

"Noted," Helena stated. "Now tell me."

"Junior has them," the captive started. "He took them to Ithaca, New York, to meet the President. And I believe Bossman is with them."

Helena's heart dropped. "All three of them are captured?" This was not good.

"That's the most recent update we received."

"How long until Chase gets to them?" Helena demanded. She needed to know how much time she had. How quickly did she need to act to save her loved ones? It couldn't end like this. They couldn't be taken away from her.

"I don't know," they sighed. "I swear."

Helena punched them in the stomach. They groaned in pain.

"I swear I don't know!"

"Then guess!"

"A few days, maybe! Chances are they're already dead!"

"Wrong answer!" Helena screamed as she plunged a knife into their gut.

The captive was stunned as they looked at her. Helena could sense a flicker of disbelief and betrayal in their eyes, as if they couldn't believe she would really kill them. Tears streamed down her face. Jade and Razor couldn't be dead. They just couldn't be. She would've heard something about it by now.

Helena closed her eyes and took a deep breath. *Focus, Helena. Focus. What does your gut tell you?*

No.

They weren't dead.

Jade wouldn't let that happen. Neither would Razor. They both understood what was at stake and would move heaven and earth to get back to her. Or more like burn heaven and earth. Either way, they wouldn't leave her here all alone.

The next step was to reach Ithaca, New York, or at least get as close as possible. She was confident she would run into them that way. Jade had a talent for escaping when she was captured, and this time should be no different. Plus, with Razor and Bossman with her, escape was almost inevitable. Helena just needed to be somewhere they could find her quickly.

"Junior is holding them in Ithaca, New York," Helena stated as two Black Coats members carried away the dead captive.

"They're in New York?!" Tatianna asked in disbelief.

Helena nodded silently.

"And Bossman is with them?" Cole asked.

Helena sighed. "Yes."

"What's the next move?" Clay demanded as he stood, his leg wobbling beneath him.

Helena noticed it. She looked him in the eyes. "It's simple. We get as close to Ithaca as possible."

"I don't think that's a good idea," Jackson stated.

"You got a better one," Helena snapped.

"We don't even know if what was said was true," Jackson retorted.

"So, what is your suggestion?!" Helena was growing tired of him. He seemed so off to her lately.

"I'm not going to let you put yourself in danger!"

"What the hell are you talking about?!"

"Jackson," Cole said, placing a hand on his son's shoulder. Jackson immediately shrugged him off.

"It's dangerous," Jackson said, locking eyes with Helena. "We need to stay put."

"I wasn't asking for your permission," Helena glared at him. "You can stay right where you are. I'm going to get my husband and sister back."

Jackson moved closer and was about to say something when Clay stepped between them. He moved so Helena would be directly behind him.

"How do we verify the information?" Clay asked.

Jackson looked at him. "We find Liam."

Helena sighed. "That's easier said than done. And we'd just be wasting time!"

Clay reached behind and touched her arm as if to say, 'Be quiet.' "Then we'll do that," he said, looking over at Reagan. "Reagan, Zara, I believe you have a lead?"

"We do," Reagan said.

"Let's move," Zara said, gathering up her weapons.

"Is that good enough for you?" Clay asked Jackson. Helena didn't miss the sarcasm in his tone.

Jackson gave a curt nod and stomped out of the building they were hiding in.

"What the hell is his problem?" Helena demanded.

Clay shrugged as he turned to her. "Overcompensating," he said, looking at Helena. "You ok?"

She sighed and nodded. "I'll be better once I get my husband and sister back."

"Me too," he said with a small smile.

"Thank you."

Clay nodded. "Let's go find Liam."

**

They were hiding inside a building that used to be an old computer store. They were on College Street—not far from headquarters on University Ave. Reagan, Danita, Keeper, and a few Black Coats members stayed behind while the group went out to find Liam. Danita's condition hadn't improved, and many of them didn't think she would make it through.

To Helena's dismay, Jackson was coming with them, along with Cole, Tatianna, Yoko, Zara, and Clay. Helena suggested that Clay stay back with Keeper because of his wonky knee, but Clay wasn't having it.

"I'm going with you," he said.

"Jade needs you," Helena said.

"The same can be said about you," he shot back.

Helena sighed. Clay had a point. There was no use arguing with him, so she gave in. Clay, she could handle. In fact, she found him very helpful and oddly comforting. Jackson, however, was a different matter. She didn't understand his urgent need to "keep her safe," but Helena didn't like it.

"You're the one who needs to stay back," Jackson grumbled when Helena said she was going with them.

"Enough!" Tatianna snapped. "Deal with your daddy issues at another time!"

Everyone looked uncomfortably between Cole and Jackson.

"Alright," Zara began. "The location is pretty obvious. And honestly, when we heard it, we kicked ourselves for not thinking of it sooner."

"Ok," Helena said. "So, where is it?"

"Sunnybrook Health Sciences Centre... or what used to be it."

"What exactly is it?" Helena asked, confused.

"I believe it's some kind of hospital, right?" Cole said.

Zara nodded.

Cole sighed as if he also should have thought of that earlier. "It makes perfect sense."

"You know how to get there from here?" Helena asked Zara.

Zara nodded once more.

"How long?"

"A couple of hours," Zara paused. "But we have to factor in the people we might meet along the way."

And the potential fights, too, Helena thought to herself. That could turn a two-hour trip into eight or an entire day. It didn't matter. They had to get moving. Time was not on their side, and she had to confirm the locations of Jade and Razor.

"Lead the way," Helena said.

"Everyone has what they need?" Zara asked the group. Everyone nodded.

"We have incoming," a member announced.

"Radicals?" Zara asked.

"Negative," the member said. "It's Brice and a few surviving members."

"Jackson, Tatianna, with me," Zara ordered. "Let's make sure they weren't followed."

Helena watched them leave. She was surprised that Brice managed to get through all of that. From what Jade and Razor told her, he seemed to have a habit of freezing up under pressure. Apparently, that wasn't the case in all situations.

"I'm sorry about Jackson's behavior," Cole said after a moment.

"It's nothing you should apologize for," Helena smiled.

"His anger towards me is showing in various ways. I hate that it's started affecting you."

"I say it's more like an obligation," Clay said. "To Jade. He feels like he failed at protecting the children, so now he's making it up by protecting Helena."

"Well, whatever it is, it's annoying," Helena watched the door, wondering when they would come in. She was more than ready to leave.

A few more seconds of silence lingered between them. Clay shifted, and Helena wondered if his leg was bothering him. Cole and Keeper managed to create a makeshift brace for him, but Helena questioned how effective it was.

"Are you really going to be ok with making this trip?" she asked.

"Yeah, I'll be fine," Clay smiled reassuringly. "Trust me, I've endured worse."

Helena nodded, but she remained unconvinced. She knew she'd need to watch him closely.

Finally, Zara and the others arrived. Brice nervously glanced around. Jackson appeared annoyed.

"Is this all that's left of us?" Brice asked, looking around the room.

"As of now," Cole stated. "We haven't had time to look for others."

Brice nodded.

"We need to know now. Are you staying or going?" Zara demanded.

"I think we should stay," Brice said, looking at the few members who were with him. They all nodded.

"Fine," Zara said. "Make sure there's a regular shift of lookouts on patrol."

"Copy that," Brice said weakly.

She didn't know why, but Helena felt sorry for Brice. Everything they had built and owned had just been destroyed. It must have been hard for him to process it. It was hard for her to process it as well, and she wasn't even there at the beginning. But so much had happened, and rescuing Jade and Razor was her top priority.

"Alright," Helena said. "Shall we get going?"

"Right," Zara said, turning away from Brice. "Let's go."

The group was silent as they walked down the road. Zara and Yoko led the way. Helena, Tatianna, and Clay followed behind, while Jackson and Cole kept at the back. Helena struggled with the feeling that there weren't enough people for this mission.

"Don't forget," Zara had said. "He's lost a lot of people, too."

Helena kept that in mind, but honestly, they were all clueless about how many people Liam might have. They just needed to catch him alone. If they could do that, they'd be in good shape. However, Helena couldn't shake the feeling that they'd end up killing Liam before extracting anything from him.

"This is pointless," Clay muttered.

Helena glanced at him, in shock.

"I don't think Liam will give us information whether he's captured or not."

"Then why did you agree to this?" Helena demanded. They could be on their way to New York by now.

"Because there'd be arguments and discourse within the group saying that we didn't 'explore all of our options.' This negates that," Clay rolled his eyes, as if he hated having to go along with it.

"I just wonder if it's worth it," Helena said. She would rather be heading to Razor and Jade right now.

"Do you really want to spend the whole trip arguing with Jackson?"

Helena sighed, realizing Clay had a point. She glanced back and noticed Jackson watching her. Quickly, she diverted her eyes back to the road ahead.

Zara suddenly stopped. The group immediately halted. Helena glanced around and listened for anything unusual. Should they take cover? She didn't notice anything strange. Nothing appeared suspicious either. But she had never been in this area before, so that meant little.

"Let's get out of sight," Zara whispered.

They all took cover in thick foliage not far from the street and waited to see if someone was coming.

"It might've been my mind playing tricks on me," Zara whispered after a moment.

Yoko shook her head. "I heard something, too. Let's wait another minute or two."

A minute later, Helena heard some chatter. It sounded like a group of people was coming their way.

"What do you think?" Helena asked Zara quietly. "Radicals?"

Zara shrugged. "You never know."

They were only a few blocks, or maybe more, away from their current hideout. Was it really too far-fetched to think that these could be Radical members? Helena wasn't sure what the best course of action was. Should they confront the group? Be prepared to fight if necessary? Should they wait until they're out of view and then continue on their journey? Or should they capture and interrogate one of them to gather some intel? Helena didn't know which option was best.

"Let's just let them pass," Helena suggested. After weighing all the options, she chose the one that would require the least effort and time from them. There was no sense in fighting when it wasn't necessary. They could save all their energy for Liam.

"Agreed," Zara said.

The group hurried on. It seemed they knew their destination. Once the mysterious group was out of sight, they waited a few minutes. Jackson checked if the road was clear. He returned and told them everything was fine.

"Alright, let's get going," Zara said. They all quickly got back on the road to Liam's hideout.

"Good call," Jackson told Helena as she walked past him.

She didn't respond. His approval didn't mean anything to her, and she sure as hell wasn't looking for it. All she wanted right now was to get to Liam and make sure that Jade and Razor were really in New York.

They all had to take cover a few more times on the road to avoid possible confrontations with another group. They set out on their journey in the early afternoon. The sun was slowly setting when Sunnybrook came into view.

"Let's go get the information we need," Helena said.

~7~

Jade

The ride was bumpy, but that didn't wake Sunday. She had cried herself to sleep as Jade comforted her in the back of the stolen DC truck. Razor told her that Sunday had killed another guy to save him. Jade didn't know how to process this information. Her body count was rising, but it wasn't like Jade could scold her for it. Sunday did what she had to do. And isn't that what Jade had wished for Raina and Levi?

Sunday's head bobbed gently as it rested on Jade's shoulder. Jade slowly moved away, giving Sunday space to lie fully on the back seat. Jade watched her carefully. Sunday looked so beautiful and carefree when she slept. Jade could see the fear and stress she tried to hide during the day, but when Sunday was sleeping, she appeared like a child again. Jade leaned down and softly kissed Sunday's forehead. Even that didn't wake her. The poor child was utterly exhausted.

"Stop worrying," Razor said, glancing back at Jade from the driver's seat. They had been driving in silence for some time now. The only sound filling the silence was Sunday's cries, which had stopped about twenty minutes ago.

"I wonder how often she's done this," Jade said. It was a question that gnawed at her mind. How many people has Sunday killed?

"It doesn't matter," Bossman interjected. "The kid knows how to keep herself alive."

"You would say that," Jade rolled her eyes, even though Bossman couldn't see her from the passenger seat.

"We can't dwell on it too much, Jade," Razor said. "This is how kids survive in this world now. They have to do the same as we do. But trust me, I don't like it any more than you do."

Jade sighed. At least there was that. Someone else felt the same kind of conflict she did. They fell back into silence. The truck kept swaying as they drove over the damaged pavement. Jade looked at Sunday again and sighed. Why did everything feel so helpless?

$**$

Razor had driven deep into the night before they stopped. They needed to find gas. If it hadn't been for that, Jade was sure Razor would've kept going until they reached headquarters.

"There's not a can in the back or something?" Jade asked. She always wondered how the DCs could drive around in their trucks for so long.

Bossman was rummaging through the trunk. He pulled out a gas can and shook it. Jade could hear the small amount of liquid inside.

"It's not enough," Bossman stated.

Jade sighed.

Razor looked around. They were just hidden behind some trees, away from the main road. "I don't think we'll find anything around here."

Bossman frowned and moved to the passenger side of the vehicle. He opened the glovebox and searched inside for a few seconds. Finally, he pulled out a map. He studied it for a while—looking for something.

Sunday, now awake from her sleep, looked over at Jade. "What's he doing?" she whispered.

Jade shrugged and looked at Razor, but he didn't seem bothered by Bossman. She paused for a few seconds before speaking.

"Care to share with the class?"

Bossman looked at her. "Stay put. I have a lead."

Jade frowned.

"How long?" Razor asked before Jade could say anything.

"Two hours at most."

Razor nodded.

Bossman quickly walked off without a word. Jade was surprised that he was willing to go alone. She also found it odd that Razor didn't suggest someone to accompany him. Was it smart for him to go solo? They didn't even know where he was headed. If something happened, they wouldn't know where to find him. Clearly, he was confident that nothing would happen. The thought annoyed Jade.

"How long before you start looking for him?" Jade asked Razor after a while.

"Three hours."

"Do you know where he's headed?"

"I have a hunch."

Sunday looked around nervously. Jade watched her closely. Sunday appeared anxious, her eyes darting around frantically.

"We're going to be fine," Jade said reassuringly.

Sunday looked at her and sighed. "I've never been this far out before."

Jade nodded. "Trust me, it's better that you stick with us."

"I know. It's just weird, that's all," Sunday scooted closer to her and rested her head on Jade's shoulder. Jade wrapped an arm around her and kissed her forehead.

Razor looked back at them. "We'll be back to Helena soon enough."

"Yeah, but we should rest once he gets back."

"You can rest now," his voice had a slight edge. "We're leaving as soon as he gets back."

"Razor, you've been driving all day. Get some rest first."

"I'm not resting until I get back," he snapped.

"How about you rest a little now?" Sunday suggested. "Jade and I can keep watch."

Razor looked at her. At first, he appeared stern, but after a few seconds, his face softened. Sunday definitely had a hold on him. He nodded.

"Wake me when he gets back or when the three hours are up," he ordered.

"Will do," Jade said.

Razor turned and rested his head on the headrest. After a few minutes, they heard him softly snoring.

"Let's go keep watch outside," Jade whispered to Sunday. Sunday nodded.

They kept the truck in view as they walked the perimeter. Jade didn't want to go too far out and made a point to avoid the main road. They remained quiet for a while. Sunday showed interest in their surroundings, as if she were seeing everything for the first time. But to

Jade, there was nothing special to see—just trees, grass, and damaged terrain.

Sunday sighed. "I really hope we don't run into anyone else out here," she said, looking at Jade, sadness in her eyes. "I don't think I can handle any more nightmares."

"Everything will be fine," Jade said. She reflected on the nightmare's statement. She used to have them, too, when she cared about the people she killed. At least there was that. Sunday felt guilty enough to have nightmares. She wasn't too far gone.

Now, Jade just needed to ensure Sunday wasn't put in another situation where she'd have to kill someone. That was easier said than done.

They patrolled for about an hour. Jade decided they would go back to the truck and limit their patrol to that area. Razor was still sleeping when they returned. Sunday sat in the back seat, the door open, with her feet dangling out. Jade leaned against the truck. It was peaceful out. It didn't seem likely they would run into anyone out here. Still, Jade felt anxious. They really needed to get back to HQ. She had to talk to Helena about what was going on. Jade hadn't had time to think about Helena's pregnancy since Sunday's been with them.

The thought never crossed her mind, but Jade was about to gain another family member. It was both terrifying and exciting. She had never seriously considered having children, as she didn't believe she was fit to raise anyone. However, Helena was stronger than she was. Helena might never realize that, but Jade always thought so. The family lineage would continue with Helena and Razor, but Jade was certain her branch in the family tree would end with her, and she was completely fine with that.

A twig snapped. Jade pushed Sunday further into the truck and quietly closed the door. Jade crouched where she couldn't be seen but was also able to keep the intruder in line of sight and the line of fire.

"It's just me," Bossman called out.

Jade rolled her eyes. She would do anything to fire a shot and take him out right now. This whole situation felt strange and unfair. Why did it have to turn out like this? Jade was determined to restore balance so she could get her revenge.

"Still determined to avenge us," Raina sighed as she appeared beside Jade. Her and Levi's appearances had been less frequent lately, especially since Sunday had been around.

"Damn straight," Jade shifted her stance. If she fired her shot, it would be lethal. There would be no way Bossman could survive it. And even better, there would be no way he could dodge it. Seriously, when would she get another chance like this again?

Bossman looked around. Razor was still asleep, and Sunday was crouched on the back floor.

"Jade," Bossman sighed. "Now is not the time."

Jade remained silent as she continued to consider her options.

"I get it," he continued. "This moment is too good to pass up, but we have bigger fish to fry right now."

You have bigger fish to fry right now, Jade thought. My biggest fish has always been you. Jade held her breath—preparing to fire.

"Jade?" Sunday whispered, her voice cracking as fear took hold.

Dammit. Jade sighed and stood up. No matter how badly she wanted to kill him, she couldn't do that in front of Sunday. She was already having nightmares. Jade didn't want to make them worse.

Bossman seemed relieved when she appeared.

"Find anything?" she asked.

He held up two gas cans. "This should be enough to get us back."

"Good," Jade said as she walked over to wake Razor while Bossman filled the tank. Neither of them spoke about the tense standoff that just happened.

Razor stepped out of the truck to stretch. Jade checked in on Sunday; she was now sitting in the backseat, resting her head against the open window.

"Sorry about that," Jade whispered.

Sunday shrugged. "We need to get back to your sister."

Jade nodded as she got ready to join Sunday in the backseat.

"For a moment there," Bossman said as he put the gas cans in the trunk. "I really thought you were going to kill me, my sweet, sweet Jade."

Razor raised an eyebrow as he looked at her.

Jade rolled her eyes. "Shut the hell up, and get in the truck."

Bossman chuckled as he closed the trunk and got in the passenger seat. Razor was still standing outside, looking at her.

"I'm fine, Razor," she sighed. "Let's just go."

Razor nodded and got in. They were back on the road almost immediately.

~8~

Clay

The uneasy feeling Clay had as they slowly approached Sunnybrook wouldn't go away. The entire compound looked unsettling, and something seemed wrong. Some buildings had barricades and appeared heavily guarded, while others looked abandoned except for minor repairs to the doors and windows. The setup was designed to make you wonder which building actually housed the leader of the Radicals. Clay had to admit, it was a clever plan. It was a good way to alert the Radicals to any intruders.

What now?" Jackson asked, annoyed. "Do we just pick a building at random?"

Zara looked around and frowned. "No, we should split up."

"That sounds like a bad idea," Jackson replied.

"If we choose the wrong building, it'll give us away," Clay said.

"If we haven't already," Helena said, annoyed.

Clay couldn't disagree with her there. They were standing out in the open discussing this plan. It wasn't their most brilliant idea.

"Let's quickly split into pairs and take a building," Cole suggested.

"Clay and I will take that building," Helena said immediately, pointing to a building near the back. It wasn't barricaded. It looked abandoned, apart from minor upkeep. Most of the windows were boarded up, except for a few. It seemed too strategic to be random.

Jackson was about to say something when Tatianna cut him off. "You can come with me and Yoko," she snapped. They headed toward a barricaded building.

Zara looked over at Helena and Clay. "Then I guess Cole and I will handle this one up front." The building she pointed to was also barricaded.

"We'll check the next building if we come up empty," Cole stated.

"Sounds good," Helena said. "Clay."

Clay nodded as he followed Helena to the back. During the time he had known her, Helena had never seemed so intense as she did now. Not when he was in prison, and she visited their cell to watch over Reagan. Not when they were at camp. Not even during their whole journey to find Blackwell. Helena had never been this intense. Clay knew they had to get back to Jade and Razor soon because, right now, the path they were on was sure to turn into a bloodbath.

They approached the front door of their building. Clay passed Helena and paused at the door.

"Let me check it out first," he said, pulling out his knife.

Helena didn't argue with him. She nodded as she moved into position to support him.

Clay sighed with relief. At least she seemed to be agreeable right now. That was a small victory. Clay slowly opened the front door — though it wasn't much good. The door wasn't locked, but it was so rusty on the hinges that it creaked loudly, and he was sure everyone nearby could hear it. It was basically an alarm announcing intruders.

"Great," Clay mumbled. He paused for a moment, watching to see if anyone would rush over to meet them.

Helena glanced around. "That was bound to alert someone."

"Still want to proceed?" He knew what her answer would be, but he just had to be certain.

"We didn't come all this way just to be driven off by a squeaky door."

"Fair enough," he took a deep breath, counted to ten, exhaled, and then stepped inside. No one had charged at them, so it was safe to assume either no one was here or the danger was deeper inside. Either way, he was ready.

Helena stayed close behind him, watching the door. There was also a chance that some Radical members might rush in after them, trapping them inside. Again, Clay was prepared for this possibility as well. But he was ready to do whatever it took if it meant finding out where Jade was.

It was exhausting to fight for so long. Ever since he and Reagan rescued that woman and her children from the DCs, it felt like they'd been fighting nonstop. Still, he didn't regret it. Not for a second. This was better than sitting back and letting something so terrible and unjust happen to people around him.

No, this new medical law didn't affect him. He and his family were the privileged ones. But still, it was only a matter of time before even the privileged were targeted and put on some enemy's list. That's why he felt the need to fight against the system. If he didn't fight now, and if others didn't fight now, they would end up in a worse mess than this. Resistance was the only way to fight back. It just pained him that his parents didn't see it the same way.

Clay wondered whether they were still alive. Health-wise, he was confident they were fine, but he wasn't so sure they had survived the many natural disasters. That was the one downfall no one, whether privileged or sick, could escape. Despite what his father believed, the survival of the fittest didn't apply to rare natural disasters that couldn't be predicted.

"It looks like this floor is clear," Helena sighed, breaking through his thoughts.

Clay looked around. He spotted a doorway that led to the staircase. "Yeah, let's head up."

"Right behind you."

The building had three floors, not counting the basement. If they found nothing on those floors, Clay would suggest checking the basement. He didn't doubt Liam might use an unorthodox method.

They slowly moved up to the second floor. Clay paused at the door and listened for any sounds. Helena stayed close behind him. He didn't hear anything, so he gently pushed the door open and waited a few seconds.

"Anything?" Helena whispered.

"One second," Clay poked his head out and looked around. He slowly walked out of the stairwell. "I think we're good."

Helena followed out. "Should we split up and check the rooms?"

"No," Clay could see it all falling apart now. "We've split up enough."

"Ok."

Again, Clay was surprised that Helena agreed. Maybe it was his tone, or perhaps it was just Jackson she wanted to oppose. Either way, Clay was grateful she wasn't resisting him. It'd make the process go a lot faster.

"I think we should start with these rooms back here and work our way down," Clay suggested. The stairwell was at the back of the hall. There were rooms directly across from it, and restrooms were next to the stairwell.

"Sounds good."

They quietly searched through the rooms. Helena kept a frown on her face the entire time. Clay could tell she was disappointed whenever they came up empty. Not that he could blame her. They had to find Liam fast. They also had to find Razor and Jade quickly. Time wasn't on their side, and it was starting to feel like everything and everyone were closing in on them.

They searched the two rooms and the men's restroom before moving toward the women's restroom. Helena checked each stall while Clay waited by the door. There were only three stalls in the bathroom. Nothing and no one was there.

Helena sighed as they left the bathroom. "What do we do if we come up empty?"

"We make our way to New York," Clay stated matter-of-factly. "With or without the group."

"You're ok with it just being us two?" she raised an eyebrow.

"We'll get there faster, I'm sure."

Helena chuckled softly. "You're right about that. Thank you, Clay. I'm starting to understand why my sister has been so attracted to you."

"I'm just trying to be helpful," Clay shrugged, though he appreciated the fact that she gave him her approval.

They reached the area in the hall with more rooms. There were six rooms on each side of the hallway. Clay sighed. If they wanted to clear this floor quickly, they would have to split up. He hated that idea.

"We can do this quickly," Helena said, her grip on her knife tightening even more.

"Alright," Clay said. "We head in at the same time and don't go to the next room until we're both back in the hall."

"Right," Helena walked over to the room across from his.

They both got into position. Clay took a deep breath and exhaled slowly. They needed to be quick and thorough, ensuring everything went smoothly.

"Go," Clay announced.

They cleared the second floor in about three minutes and moved on to the third. Each empty room pushed Clay closer to despair. Their time had been wasted—time they could have used heading to New York. He dreaded glancing at Helena. Hurt and rage painted her face. He knew she was thinking the same thing. And he was sure Jackson would endure her wrath if the others also came up empty.

"Let's head out," Clay said, but he paused at the door to the stairwell. "We could check the basement."

Helena nodded. "We need to be thorough."

Something felt off when they returned to the first floor. Clay wasn't sure what it was, but something was different than before. Maybe his mind was tricking him, or he was just being paranoid. He had a lot on his mind when they first entered this place. But still.

"Stop," Helena whispered urgently. They had just exited the stairwell. Clay paused and looked at her. "Someone's here."

"No need to play shy now," they heard a male voice say. "Come on out."

Helena's face was filled with anger as they turned the corner that concealed the stairwell from the rest of the floor. Liam stood proudly at the end of the hall, directly in front of the door they entered.

"Been hiding all this time, you coward?" Helena spat.

Liam chuckled. "There was no need. You two were so loud and obvious that I knew where you would be before you even got there."

"Where are my husband and sister?"

"Somewhere hanging in New York," Liam smirked.

Clay remembered that Liam was a good-looking guy, but was he always this short? He seemed to have gotten shorter since they last saw him. Or was Clay just trying to replace his anger with something else? Because that "hanging" comment really pissed him off. But he needed to focus on the task at hand. Like, where exactly were they in New York?

"Care to be more..." Clay couldn't finish his sentence because he couldn't understand what he was seeing.

Helena rushed past him and reached Liam before he could react. There was no time for Liam to respond. Helena's knife slashed in different directions, and the next thing he knew, Liam was on the ground, bleeding out. It all felt so surreal and terrifying. Clay didn't think even Jade would react like that.

Clay hurried over to them. Helena loomed over Liam, trembling with anger. Liam was gasping for breath as blood pooled around him. He wouldn't be alive for much longer.

"Where?" Clay asked desperately. "Where exactly in New York?"

Liam just stared at them with wide eyes as he gasped for air. The realization of his death was hitting him, and from the look on his face, he wasn't expecting it to happen today. Clay and Helena just watched as he took his final breath, and his eyes glazed over.

"Shit," Clay sighed as he looked at Liam's dead body. "That was anticlimactic."

Helena nodded as she looked around—her hands were bloody. Oddly, no one else was there. It was strange that Liam was alone. Was that intentional, or were there just fewer Radicals remaining? Clay wasn't sure if that was good or bad. With Liam gone, could they pinpoint Jade and Razor's precise location?

"Let's go," Helena finally said. "I got what I wanted from him."

Clay watched as she headed toward the door. He wasn't sure how true that statement was.

~9~

Jade

"You've got to be joking," Jade thought she had misheard what Razor and Bossman were discussing. She took a deep breath and was counting to ten when Razor's voice came through again.

"No," he sighed. "It makes logical sense."

They had just crossed into Canada when Bossman announced he had a hunch about where the Radicals were based. He proposed they capture Liam and bring him back to the Black Coats' headquarters to get information through torture.

"Razor," Jade said slowly so that he could understand her point. "We've spent all this time just trying to get back to Helena."

"I know," he groaned. He seemed to dislike the idea of a detour, but was still considering it. "But Nick has a point. We need more info, and it doesn't make sense to go back to HQ just to leave again."

"Then send Zara and Brice!" she snapped. Why was he considering this? Jade just wanted to get back to her sister.

"With Nick?" he countered.

"Who says he'll even be allowed there?!" Why did Razor choose today of all days not to make sense? "He killed Cole's daughter!"

"I didn't pull the trigger," Bossman said casually.

"But you gave the order!"

"Jade, this isn't ideal, but it has to be done," Razor said, his voice tinged with finality.

Jade closed her eyes and took deep breaths. She needed to calm down, but the thought of Bossman going to HQ with them was frustrating. Rage was flowing through her. This wasn't what she agreed to. Or was it? No. For her, the border was the furthest she was willing to go with Bossman. Taking extra trips with him in Canada wasn't part of the plan. Who cared if the President had a hit out on them? Jade didn't care. As long as she had the chance to drive her knife into Bossman's black heart, nothing else mattered.

Sunday gently rubbed Jade's back. Jade opened her eyes and looked at her. She had been silent throughout the whole ordeal. She looked afraid. Jade wondered if it was because of her anger. With that thought, she caved.

"Fine," Jade mumbled. "Let's get this over with."

"We're still a ways out," Bossman said. "We should stop and rest for the night."

"Agreed," Razor said. "There's no telling how many people we'll have to get through to reach him."

Jade blocked them out. Her emotions were all over the place, and she needed to take time to get them under control. She thought about her mention of Beverly. Why did she refer to her as Cole's daughter? For some reason, at that moment, she didn't have the heart to say her name. She hadn't thought about her much. Jade's main focus had been on dealing with the grief of losing David, Raina, and Levi; no one else had crossed her mind. Oddly enough, she was missing Beverly right now.

Mostly, she missed having someone to argue with. Beverly was always ready for a good argument, which kept Jade angry. And right now, Jade needed, no, wanted to be angry. That was something she could never get from Razor. He had a way of making sense, and his logic would eventually calm her down. That wasn't the case with Beverly. She was driven by pride and the need to save face, with no rationality behind it. That kept Jade's anger alive.

Jade sighed. What wouldn't she give to have that right now? She wasn't sure if missing Beverly this much was a good or bad thing. If she had to choose, she'd probably say the latter. But it didn't matter. Jade never pretended to be good anyway.

They drove for about 20 more minutes until Razor found a suitable spot for them to stop. It was an empty, rundown garage. Nothing too big or special, and they wouldn't need to take turns patrolling through the night. The place was so small they'd be able to hear if someone was coming, even if they were all asleep.

Jade set up her sleeping pallet in the back with Sunday. She tried to make it as comfortable as possible. She was eager to get back to HQ and sleep in a cozy bed again. Sunday quickly claimed the spot near the wall. Once Jade joined her, Sunday snuggled up to her and drifted off to sleep. Jade found it so reassuring to have her there that it frightened her. She couldn't lose this again.

"You won't," Raina's voice whispered to her. Jade couldn't see her; was she fading away, leaving her for good? The thought brought tears to her eyes.

"I miss you," Jade whispered back, wiping away her tears. Jade wrapped her arms around Sunday and fell asleep.

**

There was a time when Jade was considered a light sleeper, but that hadn't been the case recently. So, when she woke up in the middle of the night to find her arms empty and Sunday no longer beside her, panic started to set in. Jade looked over to where Razor was sleeping and saw that Sunday wasn't there either. She then glanced at the garage door, where Bossman had been, and noticed he was gone too.

Then she heard commotion outside. Jade quickly grabbed her knives and ran out. She could hear Razor stirring as she rushed out the door.

"That's it," she heard Bossman say. "Come at me just like that."

Jade rounded the corner of the garage, where she could hear Bossman's voice, and saw Sunday charging at him with a baton in her hand. Bossman quickly tossed her aside, and Sunday went tumbling to the ground. Sunday let out a small groan. The sight horrified Jade, and she charged at him immediately. She shoved him against the garage wall, with her knife at his throat. He chuckled.

"How dare you fuckin' touch her?!" Jade's hand shook as she pressed the knife closer to his throat.

"Relax, my sweet Jade," he said casually, as if he knew she wouldn't slit his throat. "She asked me to help her."

"I don't give a damn what she asked you to do! I told you not to go near her."

Bossman sighed. "Don't you think this is a little *much*?"

Jade couldn't believe he dared to say that to her. After everything he did, he still had the nerve to call her reaction "a little much." No, this wasn't enough. Anything less than killing him was definitely not enough. And that was what she was going to do.

"Bastard!"

Jade moved to slit his throat, but he saw right through her plan. He quickly headbutted her, and Jade stumbled back, dropping her knives. Bossman attempted to knee her in the stomach, but Jade dodged it. She quickly shoved him into the wall and began punching him in the gut. It didn't appear to bother him. He swiftly seized her and applied a chokehold.

"You need to calm down," he grunted.

"Stop it!" Razor immediately yelled when he rounded the corner.

Jade ignored them and elbowed Bossman in the face. He groaned as he let her go. She tackled him again, bringing him to the ground this time. They landed close to her knives. Jade pinned Bossman and swiftly grabbed a knife. Then she went in for the kill. Bossman freed an arm and grabbed her knife hand. There was a tense standoff between them. Despite his hold on her arm, Jade's knife was gradually moving toward his sternum. She just needed to be more diligent. She could do it. She could kill him. Jade just needed to push harder.

"Jade," Sunday cried. "Please stop."

Sunday's voice sounded so pained that Jade immediately looked over. Sunday was clutching Razor's arm, tears running down her face. She looked horrified.

"I'm sorry," Sunday continued. "I asked him to teach me some fighting moves even though you told me not to talk to him."

"Don't," Jade barely whispered. She felt so weak and disgusted with herself. "Don't say that."

Jade slapped Bossman's arm away. She stood up and walked over to Sunday. She crouched down in front of her.

"I'm the one who's sorry, Sunday," Jade said. "I shouldn't have scared you like that."

Sunday responded by hugging Jade. Jade clung tightly to her, her thin frame trembling with fear. Jade hated herself for causing Sunday to feel that way. Who was she becoming? Or more accurately, what had she become?

"Let's get back to bed," Jade suggested.

Sunday nodded.

Jade rose and took Sunday's hand. Bossman approached her, holding the knives. He stopped in front of her and handed them over. Jade snatched them from his hand.

"We good?" The anger was clear in her tone.

Bossman smirked. "For now."

"Sounds good to me," Jade said, feeling very satisfied with that comment. It made it clear that they both knew this moment of truce was only temporary. He should never forget that.

**

The sign on the building read: *M Wing, Main Entrance, Sunnybrook Health Sciences Centre.* The place was a hospital. *A hospital.* This was where Bossman led them. Jade stared at the sign as she tightened her grip on her knife. The main hospital was huge, plus there were multiple buildings on the property.

"Please tell me you have a hunch about which building it might be," Jade said, annoyed.

"Sorry, my love, I can't," he sighed.

"I'm not your fuckin' love!"

"Quiet," Razor snapped. He was annoyed with her after last night.

Jade felt a little guilty, but not enough to ease her anger. Sunday looked around, her eyes flicking over everything. She was holding Jade's hand, and Jade noticed it tighten.

"Judging by how this building is boarded up," Razor said, looking at the hospital's main entrance. "I'd say we'll have better luck with the surrounding buildings. We can search the hospital if we come up empty everywhere else."

"Agreed," Bossman said. "Let's get on with it."

"Should we split up?" Jade asked Razor. "It'll speed things up."

"One of us would be stuck with a child," Razor said, looking at her as if she were stupid.

"I'm useful!" Sunday snapped at him.

"I'll take that building," Bossman pointed to a building a block down from the main campus. "You three can take the building across the street."

Jade was about to shoot off a rebuttal, but stopped herself. It was pointless.

"We'll meet at the crosswalk when we're finished," Razor pointed to the crosswalk that was between the two buildings.

"Roger that," Bossman said as he walked toward his building.

Although the buildings they searched were smaller than the hospital, they still felt large. It took Jade, Razor, and Sunday nearly 40 minutes to clear them. They waited an extra 20 minutes at the crosswalk for Bossman to finish his.

"On to the next one," he announced, coming out empty-handed.

They rounded a bend to see a smaller building across from the building Bossman had just come out of.

"Let's do this one together," Razor suggested. "It's small enough so that we can clear it in a few minutes."

Jade sighed. "I hope this whole thing doesn't take up the whole day."

"It'll take as long as it takes," Razor shot back.

Yup, he was still mad at her.

The small building was boarded up, but it didn't look abandoned. The way the windows were boarded up seemed way too strategic for Jade's liking. Someone was definitely hiding out here. Bossman took the lead, followed by Razor, then Sunday. Jade took the rear. Bossman paused at the door, holding up three fingers and slowly dropping them to one. He quickly opened the door, and the creak was so loud that Jade was sure it was deliberate—like an alarm system.

"Well, the Radicals know we're here now," she grumbled.

Bossman rushed inside, and so did the others. Jade ran in only to almost tumble over Sunday. They had abruptly stopped and were looking down at something. Jade maneuvered over to get a better view.

There he was... Liam. He was lying on the ground, blood pooling around him. His lifeless eyes stared up at them.

"Well...fuck," Bossman sighed. "Looks like someone else got to him."

Jade wasn't sure if she was happy or pissed that she wasn't the one to kill him. It was definitely the latter. Either way, that was one less enemy she had to deal with.

~10~

Helena

It was as if everyone around her was speaking gibberish. Helena couldn't focus on the debate the others were having because she was fighting a wave of nausea. Keeper had given her something for the "morning sickness," although Helena wasn't sure if what she was feeling was due to the baby or the knowledge that she had killed their only lead. Make no mistake, Liam needed to die, but Helena should have gotten more information out of him first.

Silver lining: Clay was clearly defending her reaction to the others. He told the group that it didn't matter if they tortured Liam; he wouldn't give them any more information than he already had. Clay pushed for them to go to New York. Now, Helena finally understood why Jade had been so drawn to him.

"They can be anywhere in New York!" Jackson shouted for what felt like the hundredth time.

"This is no longer a discussion," Clay said in a tone that showed his mind was made up. "Helena, Reagan, and I will leave for New York tomorrow morning."

Clay looked at her for confirmation. Helena nodded with relief, feeling so happy that Clay was standing his ground for her. Right now, she was so scared that if she spoke, she might vomit.

"I will go as well," Cole said. "Helena needs a doctor nearby."

"I go where the doc goes," Zara crossed her arms.

Everyone else agreed to go too. Jackson looked around at them all, shaking his head in disapproval.

"This is stupid," he grumbled.

"You're welcome to stay here," Tatianna countered. "No one is forcing you to come along."

"Being separated doesn't seem good at this point," Cole sighed.

Jackson mumbled something under his breath and walked out of the computer store. No one stopped him. Helena sighed and closed her eyes. She understood Jackson's anger. He'd been shot, unconscious for so long, only to come out of it and find out that his sister had died and the father he thought was dead was now, in fact, alive. That whole ordeal could make anyone angry. However, he still needed to get it together.

Could she really say that? She had played a part in faking Blackwell's death. And it wasn't as if she was in complete control of her emotions either. Pot meets kettle. She planned to make everything right with him after she got Razor and Jade back.

"Again, I'm sorry for my son's behavior," Cole said sadly.

"There's no need to apologize," Helena managed to say. The nausea was spiraling out of control.

Clay handed her a bucket. Helena nodded in thanks.

"Are the pills not working?" Cole asked, alarmed.

Helena shook her head. She firmly believed that other factors were at play. The overwhelming anxiety from not having her husband and sister was taking a toll on her. She needed to gain control of it.

Brice, who had been lingering in the back of the computer store, came over to them. "Well, if we all plan on heading to New York, I think we need to go out and gather supplies."

"That's a good idea," Zara stated.

"You have a place in mind?" Cole asked.

"HQ," Brice stated. "I believe there's still plenty there that can be salvaged."

"Sounds good," Cole said, sounding impressed by the idea.

"Great, I'll gather some people to go with me. We'll take as much as we can get," Brice said as he walked off to find volunteers.

"Speaking of people for a trip," Clay said. "How's Danita doing?"

They hadn't received any updates on her. Helena was grateful that Clay asked. She wondered if they would need to take turns carrying Danita to New York, just like they did with Jackson. She hated to think it, but that would slow down their journey more than she liked. It was a terrible thought.

Cole's entire demeanor shifted. He appeared sad. "Not good, I'm afraid."

"How bad is it?" Clay asked.

"It'll be," Cole paused, as if he was searching for the right words to say. "Best if we just put her out of her misery," he finally said.

And then Helena released everything she felt into the bucket.

~11~

Razor

Distraught didn't begin to describe how Razor felt as he looked at the rubble that had once been HQ. What happened here? How long had it been like this? Were there any survivors? Razor could see charred and uncharred, dead bodies scattered around. Some were Black Coat members he recognized; others, he didn't know. But if he had to guess, he'd say they were Radical members. This was all so wrong, so very wrong. Helena was supposed to be here waiting for him. They had so much to discuss... so much to do.

Razor sank to his knees. This couldn't be real. It had to be a nightmare.

He even slapped himself a few times just to be sure. But what he saw was real. The place that held his wife and unborn child was barely standing. Karma was finally catching up to him.

"What the hell is going on?" Jade whispered. Razor could hear the distress in her voice as well.

"What happened?" Sunday asked, looking around.

"We need to move," Nick stated.

"Are you fuckin' kidding me?!" Jade's expression shifted from heartbroken to furious in seconds. "We need to find out what happened to Helena!"

"We won't get that information by standing here gawking at a decimated building."

"I'm so sick of you!" Jade pulled out a knife.

"This again," Nick sighed. "Seriously, Jade, this is getting old."

"Enough of your shit!" Razor shouted. "Both of you!"

"Razor..."

"I don't want to hear it, Jade!" Razor stood, glaring at her. "We get it, you want to kill him. But enough!"

"Maybe we can check the surrounding buildings and see if you come across someone you know," Sunday suggested. She looked nervously between them all.

"The kid gets it," Nick chuckled.

At that moment, Razor felt deeply thankful for her. The statement appeared to settle everyone down. Jade nodded in agreement.

"Thank you, Sunday," Razor smiled at her. "That's a good idea."

Jade looked around for a moment. "Which one first?"

Razor paused for a moment. He glanced at the building next to HQ and saw some significant damage. He wasn't sure how stable it was. Then he looked at the building across the street. It seemed that a small part of the blast had reached it, but not much. It looked promising, and it was more discreet than the other nearby buildings.

"Let's try here," he pointed to the building. They all started walking toward it.

"Razor?" they heard someone call out. Razor turned toward the voice. It was Keeper.

Jade immediately ran to him and threw herself into his arms. A small spark of hope started to grow in Razor's chest. Brice, Yoko, and a few other members were with Keeper, but Razor didn't see Helena.

"She's safe," Keeper told him as he released Jade from his hug. "We're holed up in an old storefront a few blocks from here."

Every muscle in Razor's body relaxed. Helena was safe. He thanked the universe and whatever higher being out there for that.

"What happened here?" Jade asked. "And why come back?"

Keeper didn't answer her questions. Instead, his hand went to the handle of the mini-axe he had sheathed at his hip for safety. He looked between Razor and Nick. "Interesting company ya keep these days."

Jade snorted. "Not by choice. He was captured with us," she looked over at Nick, and rolled her eyes. "But we wouldn't have escaped and gotten back here without him."

"We have a bigger enemy to focus on," Nick said.

"I don't think ya victims would agree."

"Look, Keeper, I get it." Razor wasn't interested in debating at the moment. All he wanted was to get back to Helena. "But can you take me to Helena first?"

Keeper looked at him, then at the rubble of the building. He walked over and picked something up. The others followed his lead, making sure they kept their distance from Nick. Keeper inspected the object for a moment and then placed it in the bag he was carrying. Razor realized they had come back to salvage some supplies.

"After Zara came back to tell us ya were captured," Keeper finally said. "The Radicals attacked while we were getting ready to head out."

Razor looked at the destroyed building again, thinking about the chaos and fear they all must have felt in that moment. He hated that Helena had to go through that without him. Keeper went back to gathering and inspecting potential supplies, with Jade and Sunday helping. Keeper didn't speak again until after adding a few more items to his bag.

"Helena had captured and tortured a Radical member for information. They told her that ya both were in New York."

"You let her torture someone?" Razor couldn't hide his anger.

"She insisted on doing it," Keeper shot back. "Ya didn't see what she was like."

"Scary," Yoko chimed in. "I didn't think she had that kind of rage in her."

"What?" Jade gasped as something hung in her hand.

It was even more urgent for Razor to reach her, but he couldn't rush. Keeper was usually relaxed, calm, and rational. But not right now. Razor could feel the hostility coming off him. He noticed the deadly looks he shot at Nick. Keeper was planning his move, positioning himself to strike at Nick. Razor had to keep everyone calm in this moment.

"Anyway," Keeper resumed, focusing on something, his stance even closer to Nick than it had been before. "Jackson convinced Helena to verify the intel by finding Liam."

"I assume Mrs. Thompson left him in that ill-fated state we found him in," Nick said to Razor, keeping a close eye on Keeper.

"Clay told us she killed Liam after he confirmed ya both were in New York... although, he didn't specify which city."

"Keeper," Razor sighed as Keeper assumed an attack stance. "Please, don't do this. We need to get back to figuring out our next plan, and I'd really love to see my wife now."

Keeper was silent as he stared at Nick. His bag was slung over his back, and he was slowly unsheathing his axe. Nick chuckled as Jade flanked him, preparing for her own attack. This wasn't something Razor wanted to deal with. Sunday slowly backed away from them. She looked over at Razor, wondering what she should do.

"We got all we could salvage for now," Brice stated. "Let's handle this back at the store, Keeper."

Keeper was silent for a few more seconds. "Go," he said, gripping the handle of his axe. "Warn them. Tell Helena to wait outside the building with Clay and Reagan."

"Copy," Brice and the others headed out. Yoko stayed behind to support.

"Make ya-self useful," Keeper said to Nick. "Help us find some more supplies."

"So you can drive that axe into my back?" Nick chuckled.

"I'll aim for ya head."

Nick laughed even harder. "That would be the right thing to do."

"But I think killing ya should be a group effort."

"You all can certainly try," Nick sighed, looking through the wreckage.

They all aimlessly searched through the rubble, picking up random items they thought might be useful. Razor didn't participate in the search. He was too busy watching over them, ensuring no one made a move. This tense moment lasted about 20 minutes.

"Alright," Keeper finally said. "Let's get this disaster reunion over with."

Keeper led them to a road called College Street. The street was lined with storefronts, many of which were in poor shape. It seemed like forever walking down that street until Keeper finally stopped right in front of a tram stop. Helena, Clay, and Reagan were standing in the middle of the street, two stores away.

Razor was at the back of the group with Nick. Helena sprinted toward them, quickly hugged Jade, and then ran to jump into Razor's arms. He caught her easily and buried his face in her hair.

"God, I missed you," he said as her scent flooded his senses.

"You scared me," her voice cracked.

Razor quickly grabbed her face and kissed her. Helena responded passionately. Razor held her tighter—the feeling of being home was overwhelming. For a frightening moment, he thought he might not make it back to her. Luckily, he did.

"You bastard!" Jackson yelled as he lunged at Nick.

Instinctively, Razor pushed Helena behind him. Sunday, who was close to Jade, ran over and took his hand.

"Are we in danger?" Sunday whispered to him. Her eyes were filled with panic as her free hand hovered over her knife, sheathed in her belt loop.

"No," Razor sighed. "But things could get a little messy."

Nick and Jackson were exchanging blows while Keeper and Jade circled them. Clay, Reagan, and Yoko stayed on the sidelines. Razor saw a group of people coming out of a store with a blue and yellow sign. He recognized Cole, Zara, Brice, and some others. Tatianna burst out and immediately went slashing at Nick just as Jackson was getting tired. That was Keeper's cue to jump in. He started swinging his axe at Nick. Nick dodged every attack easily.

"Who's this?" Helena asked, looking at Sunday.

Razor never took his eyes off the fight. "Helena, this is Sunday. Sunday, this is my wife and Jade's sister, Helena. We met Sunday in New York.

She's the reason I was able to make it back to you."

"It was nothing," Sunday said sheepishly.

"I still want to thank you, Sunday," Helena smiled. "You brought my husband and sister back to me."

Jackson had caught his breath and hurried back into the fight. "You have the nerve to show your face here!" One of Jackson's punches connected with Nick's jaw.

Nick spat out blood. "Nothing I've done was personal," he responded with a punch to Jackson's stomach and evaded Keeper's swing of his axe.

"It felt very personal!" Tatianna shouted. She lunged at him with her knife. Nick barely caught it before it reached his stomach.

Razor wondered whether he genuinely didn't see it coming or if he felt guilty about what he had done. Tatianna's prison experience was brutal because Nick arranged a hit on her. How could she not take it personally? Jade saw that moment as a chance to jump in. She wrapped her arm around Nick's neck as Tatianna pushed the knife in deeper. Sunday gasped at the sight. Nick twisted Tatianna's wrist, and the knife scraped his side. He quickly slapped Tatianna and then threw Jade over his shoulder. She hit the ground hard.

"Jade!" Sunday screamed.

"Don't worry," Razor said. "She'll be ok."

"Um, he doesn't intend to kill them, right?" Helena asked cautiously.

"No," Razor sighed. "He needs us. But it's best to let them get this out of their system."

Keeper and Jackson pressed hard on Nick, while Tatianna and Jade (who was back on her feet) slipped in to strike him. The plan was working. But Nick refused to back down, and fatigue was starting to wear everyone down. The fight felt like it lasted forever, but Razor didn't make a move. He was drained from intervening and telling everyone to stand down. Everyone had reason to be mad at Nick, as he was the cause of much of their pain. Still, Razor was exhausted from fighting, and they needed Nick for the fight to end.

In the end, no one was killed. Nick was lying in the street, chuckling while bleeding from the many cuts he'd received from Jade and Tatianna. Jackson and Keeper were kneeling on the ground, catching their breath. Tatianna was pacing, furiously wiping her tears. Jade had her hands on her knees as she focused on her breathing.

"Are you finished?" Razor finally asked.

"For now," Jade said breathlessly.

"You're damn right it's for now!" Tatianna exclaimed.

Cole cleared his throat as he stepped into the street. "Nick, what brings you here?"

"Well, Dr. Cole Blackwell," Nick winced as he sat up to look at Cole. "If you're ready to put an end to all this, then I have a proposal for you."

~12~

Jade

Bossman winced as Cole jabbed the needle into him. Jade felt a sense of satisfaction watching this. They were all in the old computer store, where Cole had Bossman lying on a desk while he stitched up the numerous cuts Jade and Tatianna had managed to land during their fight. Bossman was bleeding heavily, but not enough to satisfy her.

Clay stood directly across from her, within her line of sight. She wanted to hug him when she first saw him, but hesitated in Bossman's presence. The last thing she wanted was to repeat what happened with David. But as Jade looked at Clay, she suddenly realized how much she missed him. She'd caught his eye, and he quickly gave her a slight nod. Jade looked over at Bossman. He was watching Cole stitch one of his cuts.

"Care to elaborate on this proposal?" Jade asked, folding her arms. Her time around him really needed to come to an end.

"Yeah...gah!" he groaned, glaring at Cole. "If I didn't know any better, I'd say you're making this painful on purpose."

"You would be correct," Cole said casually. He shifted the needle slightly, causing Bossman to jerk from the pain. "Did you forget that you're the reason my daughter is dead?"

"No," Bossman gritted.

"Just because I decided to help you doesn't mean I'll make it painless."

Jade smirked. She didn't realize Cole could be so callous. "So, the plan?"

"We need to get back to Michigan," Bossman stated.

"Because?" Jade was getting annoyed that she had to draw it out of him.

"That's how we can take down Chase."

Jade sighed with frustration. Why couldn't he just explain himself? She wasn't sure if he was giving short answers because of the pain or if he wanted her to talk more, but Jade was done waiting.

"With prison breaks or the government officials?" Razor asked. It seemed like he knew what Bossman was getting at. She just wished they'd care enough to spell it out to them.

"Both," Bossman said.

"We still don't understand what the two of you are talking about," Jade pointed out.

"The officials never cared for Chase's leadership," Razor explained. "They've been looking for ways to get rid of him, but he's never given them any reason to."

"A string of prison breaks would give them a reason," Bossman said.

"Why Michigan? Wouldn't DC be better?" Jade wasn't sure if she could handle going back to Michigan.

"You'd think, but no," Razor said.

"Actually... son of a bitch!" Bossman shouted.

"Last one," Cole said casually as he swiftly moved the needle.

"Your bedside manner sucks, doc."

"Only you receive this special treatment, Nick."

Bossman chuckled, then looked back at Jade. "Michigan has a special attachment to Chase. He considers it his hometown since he went to medical school at the University of Michigan."

"All done," Cole said, grabbing his supplies and heading to the back of the store. He was still within earshot of the group.

"But will a series of prison breaks be enough? Wouldn't DC have larger numbers?" Jade asked.

"No," Bossman winced as he sat up. "Michigan houses the most medical debtors in the country. It's because the DC officers are more aggressive. Since Chase has roots there, the state wanted to ensure that the President looked good. So, a heavy breach there will weaken him."

"Ironically enough," Razor said. "Michigan is also the state with the most government officials who hate him and want to overthrow him."

"They have a helluva way of showing it," Jade grumbled.

Razor shrugged. "No one wants to get arrested for treason."

"The better question is, do we have enough people?" Helena asked, looking around the group.

Jade nodded. "That is a good question."

Bossman got off the table. "We'll take a page out of my old pal's playbook," he said, slapping Razor on the shoulder. "We'll raid the sweeps."

"That doesn't mean they'll fight with us," Tatianna spat. "Especially with *you*."

"My lovely Jade can give them a dazzling speech on why they should fight," Bossman smiled.

Jade rolled her eyes. "I think the doc is better suited for that," she grumbled.

"Even better!" Bossman laughed. "He does have a way of gathering a following."

"As long as we can put an end to this madness," Cole sighed. "Then I'm in."

"Great, we'll scavenge supplies and vehicles, then head to Michigan," Bossman said as he headed for the door.

"Going somewhere?" Cole asked sharply.

Bossman smirked. "Surely you don't expect me to lay my head where everyone wants to kill me."

"It'll make it easy for us," Cole chuckled.

"Don't wander too far," Jade demanded. Although she hated having him around, she didn't trust him to be left alone to his own devices.

"Not to worry, my love, I won't wander too far."

"I'm not your fuckin' love!" Jade glared at him as he walked out the door, wishing for the day when she could finally drive her knife into his heart.

~13~

Clay

The little girl Jade introduced Clay to was named Sunday. She was small and thin, with a frown on her face. Clay could see she was trying to seem tough, but to him, she just looked scared. This was the girl who traveled with Jade, Razor, and Bossman. The idea intrigued him. Maybe the little girl wasn't as frightened as she seemed.

"Nice to meet you," Clay smiled.

Sunday frowned even more deeply. She looked over at Jade. "I'm going to see if Razor needs me for anything."

"Ok," Jade said. She glanced back at Clay once Sunday was out of earshot. "Sorry, I think she's a little overprotective."

"It's fine," Clay managed to say before Jade rushed into his arms. She held him tight. Clay embraced her.

"I missed you," she whispered. Clay noticed the crack in her voice.

"You had me worried there," he admitted.

"Same," she whispered as her grip on him tightened. The action caused Clay's heart to race even faster in his chest.

"I'm glad you could make it back."

It was a while before Jade spoke. She had slowly pulled away from his embrace to look at him. "It was tough. Teaming up and traveling with Bossman was very taxing...it still is."

"I can only imagine."

"Well, you won't be imagining it for too long."

Clay sighed and looked around. "You want to find a place to sleep?"

Jade nodded. "Where's your setup?"

"You and Sunday want somewhere close," he stated. He couldn't assume she'd want to share a sleeping space with him. Jade had been away from him for a while now. She was able to fall asleep without him. She didn't really need him anymore.

"Oh, um," she looked down at her feet and bit her bottom lip. She was embarrassed. She kept her eyes on her feet. "I thought I'd just share a space with you...if you don't mind."

"Sure," Clay fought to keep the smile off his face.

He led her outside and through a door right next to the computer store. They climbed a flight of stairs and entered the space. It looked like it used to be some sort of communal office area. They weaved between old desks and chairs, and he led her into one of the many glass meeting rooms. His sleeping pallet was against the back wall. Jade glanced around for a moment, then began to take off her boots, unsheathed her weapons, and placed all her items next to Clay's.

Clay sat on his pallet and watched Jade move around, getting comfortable. She paused briefly, her hand hanging over the button on her pants.

"You got something I can sleep in?"

"Shirts are in that bag," Clay nodded toward a corner in the room.

Jade walked over and grabbed a shirt. She looked out the glass wall. "Should I expect someone walking in soon?"

Clay shrugged. Jade smiled as she started to change. Instinctively, Clay looked down at his hands, trying to give her some privacy. He didn't understand why he felt so shy all of a sudden. Jade was never shy about changing in front of him. But now, it felt wrong—like it was invading her privacy. Was it because of their time apart? Or was it something else— like his feelings for her changing?

He always found Jade attractive. He admired how strong and independent she was. After David's and the children's deaths, he genuinely just wanted to be there for her. But now, everything felt different. With her being captured and uncertain if she'd return to him, Clay's feelings for her deepened. He was used to just being close... friends. But now, it seemed he wanted more. Could this be love?

"Finally," Jade sighed as she sat next to him. "I feel like I can relax a little."

"I'm sure that was difficult to do with Bossman around."

"You have no idea. I couldn't take my eyes off him. Especially with Sunday around."

"She must be tough."

Jade frowned, appearing worried. "She was on her own. She had to do some difficult things to survive."

Clay nodded. He didn't need her to clarify any further. "Want to lie down?"

"Will you join me?"

"Of course," Clay waited for Jade to get comfortable before he joined her. She quickly laid her head on his chest as he wrapped his arms around her. "So, how old is Sunday? She looks pretty young."

"She says she's nine."

"It sounds like you don't believe her."

"I don't know," Jade sighed. "I don't want to think she's younger than that."

Clay nodded. It was a frightening thought that Sunday could be any younger. Jade didn't say it, but Clay knew that Sunday must have taken lives to be here today. There was simply no way someone, not even a child, could go this long without their hands being bloody. The idea saddened him. And Clay knew it saddened Jade, too.

Silence settled between them. It wasn't the awkward kind; it felt more natural. Clay concentrated on Jade's breathing, listening to the sound of it. He took in how she felt in his arms, noting the smooth and soft texture of her skin against his. He also noticed her scent. She was always fighting, so a faint smell of sweat lingered—yet it smelled sweet. Clay found it strangely comforting. He had missed that smell.

"What's on your mind?" she asked.

"Did you hear about Danita?" he didn't want to elaborate on just how much he missed her.

"Yes," she sighed. "I don't want to think about any more losses right now."

"Fair enough," Clay understood her sentiment. "How do you really feel about Bossman's plan?"

"Unfortunately, he makes a valid point. The President seems to be the real enemy here, and if we have a chance to overthrow him, then we should."

"The prison breaks would definitely free a lot of innocent people."

"That's true," she sighed. Clay enjoyed the feel of her breath against his skin. "It's just…"

"Working with Bossman isn't ideal," he said, finishing her thought.

"Exactly."

"Focus on saving the debtors and the providers. That's the reward we get for temporarily working with Bossman."

"That's a good point," she paused. "But please, be careful around him. I don't want him to know I'm close to you."

"Understood," Clay wished he knew exactly what she meant by that.

"And I appreciate you looking out for Helena."

"It was nothing."

"It was everything. She said she wouldn't have made it without you."

"I'm glad I was helpful to her."

Jade looked up at him, her eyes revealing something he couldn't understand. It didn't take long for him to realize what it meant. Jade's gentle lips pressed against his. Clay was momentarily stunned, but only briefly. He parted his lips, inviting her tongue in. His heart pounded. Yes, this was love. He just hoped it didn't doom them.

~14~

Jade

No matter how hard she tried to focus, Jade couldn't get her kiss with Clay out of her mind. It was never her intention to turn their relationship into something more intimate. But realizing how much she missed him and hearing how much he was there for Helena, emotions took over, and Jade couldn't control herself. Now she was feeling nothing but excitement, fear, and regret. Excited that after everything, she could feel something like romance again. Fearful of how it's going to end. And regretful for feeling like she'd moved on so quickly.

"Should we check in here?" Helena asked the group, pointing to an old store.

They were all currently separated into small groups to scavenge. Jade was with Helena, Tatianna, Sunday, and Keeper. They were searching the buildings near the computer store. Cole insisted that Helena stay close to their current headquarters in case she suddenly feels ill.

"Couldn't hurt to try," Tatianna said.

"Jade and I will check it first," Keeper stated.

"Me too," Sunday added.

"No," Jade said before Sunday could go on. "Stay here and watch Helena for me."

Sunday was about to object, but suddenly stopped. She frowned and nodded.

"You know I'm not a child, right?" Helena crossed her arms.

"I know," Jade looked at her sister. "But it'll make me feel better if you stay put."

"Yeah, yeah," Helena sighed.

Keeper and Jade entered the small building, with Keeper leading the way. Jade didn't have high hopes that they would find anything. But it didn't hurt to try. Plus, she needed to do something to take her mind off things, like Clay being in a group with Bossman, for example. The idea of Clay being around Bossman made Jade anxious. She couldn't let his fate end like David's. Jade would never bounce back from that.

On the bright side, Clay wasn't alone with Bossman. Razor was with them, and so was Reagan. Reagan insisted on joining her brother, maybe sharing the same worry as Jade. Either way, it brought some comfort to Jade.

"I know what you're thinking," David said as he appeared beside her. "Will that be enough?"

"It's all clear," Keeper said, glancing at Jade. "I'll go get them."

Jade nodded and watched Keeper walk away. "I can't help it," she said once she was alone. "I need to keep him safe."

"It'll be ok, Jade."

"You don't know that for sure," Jade paused. It had been so long since she had seen him. It had been a while since she'd seen Raina, and even longer for Levi. Were they upset with her? Or were they finally moving on? "Are you angry with me?"

"Of course not."

"But you don't come around anymore," Jade's voice cracked.

"Because you don't need us anymore."

"I'll always need you, David."

"Jade?"

Jade quickly spun around and saw Sunday standing behind her, looking worried. Tatianna, Keeper, and Helena all appeared uneasy. They overheard her talking to herself. Great. That "Jade's gone crazy" look was back. This was going to be fun for her.

"I'm fine," she said before anyone could ask.

"You think any of the others will find a working vehicle?" Tatianna asked as she opened the drawers of an old desk. Jade was grateful for her.

"I hope so," Helena sighed. "I really don't feel like making that long trek to Lansing on foot."

"I'm sure they'll find something," Jade said as she avoided everyone's looks.

Everyone was divided into small groups: Razor, Bossman, Clay, and Reagan formed one group. Jackson, Cole, Zara, and Yoko made up another. Brice and the other members of the Black Coats were in the last group. Jade was confident that Brice's team would find at least a couple of vehicles. They had a van when they captured Crimson, so that was at least one working vehicle. She believed he knew the locations of others.

Jade and the rest of the group fell silent as they searched through the store for supplies. Sunday was always close by her, and Jade could feel her gaze occasionally. Jade knew Sunday had some lingering questions she wanted to ask. She ignored the feeling and focused on the task at hand. She didn't find anything good—just some screws, nails, and bolts. Jade took the stuff anyway, knowing Keeper could find some use for it.

"Um, Jade," Sunday finally said.

"Hmm."

"Who's David?"

Jade could hear the others go still. The tension lingered in the air. "Someone I loved," Jade said after a moment. "And someone Bossman killed."

"Is that what happened to Raina and Levi, too?"

Jade froze. She tried to remember if she had ever said their name in front of Sunday before.

"You call out for them in your sleep," Sunday explained.

A few tears fell. Jade quickly wiped them away. "Yes, he killed them too," Jade looked over at Sunday. "Now do you understand why I say stay away from him?"

Sunday nodded. "I'm sorry."

"I know you want to be stronger," Jade sighed. "I just worry."

Sunday remained silent, fidgeting with something out of Jade's view.

"Since we're asking questions, I have a few," Jade said.

Sunday's mood lifted. "Shoot."

"How do you know so much about Snatchers' Row?"

"Snatchers' Row?" Tatianna snorted.

"What the hell is that?" Helena asked.

"It's a place in New York where women and children are sold," Sunday explained.

"The hell!" Tatianna snapped in anger.

"You were there?!" Helena said as she marched over to Sunday.

"Yes, but only to save someone," Sunday quickly said.

"Who?" Jade asked.

"I didn't really know her," Sunday shrugged. "She escaped when I met her. I think she was a teenager. She didn't talk much. But she was the first person I came across since Vivian and the gang were killed."

"You mentioned that before. How did they die?" Jade wondered.

Sunday froze. "I don't wanna talk about that."

"Ok…" Jade was at a loss for words.

"Anyway, I met her and suggested we stick together. I think that lasted about a month, until we ran into some snatchers," Sunday paused. She sat on top of a desk. "The asshole dickwads seemed to know her."

"Wow," Helena said.

"Such vulgar language," Tatianna gasped.

"Well, that's what they were!" Sunday said defensively. "Anyway, they were on us. I was close to being captured first when she just gave up. They suddenly focused on her, and I was able to escape."

Sunday looked away from the group, her mind elsewhere. Jade wondered what it was like for her to escape from something so horrible all the time. It could be daunting.

"They didn't notice it, but I followed them," Sunday continued. "I saw them take her to this house on Snatchers' Row, and I watched them for days. When the time was right, I broke in and rescued her. I wanted to save more, but I only saw her."

Sunday was quiet for a moment. Guilt washed over her face. After a few seconds, she looked at Jade. "I had to use my knife on a couple of guys."

Jade nodded in understanding.

"Where is she now?" Keeper asked, sounding very interested in her story.

Sunday shrugged. "Don't know. We were together for a couple of weeks, and then one day I woke up and she was gone."

"Did it look like there had been a struggle?" Tatianna asked.

"No," Sunday said. "All of her things were gone, too."

Silence settled over the group. Jade hoped the girl was still alive and safe somewhere.

"I like to think," Sunday finally said, "that she's in a different state, living safely with a large group."

Helena smiled. "I'm sure she is. You're really brave, Sunday."

Sunday's face lit up. "That's what I hope to be."

Jade smiled. Although her worries about Sunday's safety would never disappear, Jade was confident that Sunday would fight tooth and nail to survive. That fact brought her comfort.

~15~

Clay

Eyes were on him, but it didn't take much for Clay to realize whose they were. It was Bossman. It seemed like he couldn't take his eyes off Clay. It also didn't take much for Clay to understand why Bossman was so fixated on him. He didn't know how, but somehow Bossman figured out that he was close to Jade. That was going to be a problem. Clay couldn't let Jade worry about him. He had to watch himself.

Reagan approached him. Clay noticed how she was directly blocking Bossman's view. Maybe that's why she was so eager to join them. Clay didn't want his sister near Bossman. He didn't want anyone around Bossman—not even himself. But someone had to join Razor's group. It wasn't fair for Razor to be the only one dealing with Bossman's presence.

"There's nothing useful here," Reagan said casually, in her usual nonchalant manner.

"Excuse me, dear," Bossman said to Reagan. "But you're blocking the view."

Reagan glared at him and rolled her eyes. "Which is precisely why I decided to stand here."

Bossman chuckled. "You're an interesting one."

"Focus," Razor snapped. "Now is not the time for your antics, Nick."

"I'm just sizing up the competition," Bossman shrugged.

"The choice is clear," Reagan said. "There is no competition. Now, where's your lead on a truck?"

"I like you," Bossman smirked. "We're close."

Bossman took the lead as they headed toward a heavily wooded area. Clay was hesitant about following him, but Razor didn't seem to hesitate in following Bossman, so Clay went along. They had the upper hand over Bossman. He needed their cooperation more than ever. He would ruin that if he harmed any of them and angered Jade even more. Without Jade's cooperation, there was no group. There was no plan. And Bossman would be on the run forever. So, there was that. Still, that didn't bring Clay much comfort.

If he were being honest with himself, Clay would've preferred to be with Jade. Or, at least, with Cole's group. They were at the remains of HQ. Apparently, Razor had hidden the DC truck they drove back to Toronto there. Cole said he knew where to get more gas, so his group went to retrieve the truck and supplies from that location. He wasn't sure where Brice and his group had gone, but Clay had already had his fill of traveling with Brice.

"Don't drop your guard," Reagan whispered as she walked beside him.

Bossman and Razor were in front.

Clay nodded.

"It's interesting, you just got here and somehow you already know about this place," Reagan stated. It was clear that she was suspicious of Bossman's lead.

"Foresight, my dear," Bossman said casually. "I scouted these out before I was captured."

"Convenient."

"Indeed, it is."

"You sure it's still there?" Razor asked.

"There's only one way to find out," Bossman shrugged.

So, this had been Bossman's plan all along. He always intended to come to them and the Black Coats. If everything had gone differently, Clay wondered if they would have agreed to work with him. He really wished it had played out differently.

It seemed like their location was the farthest from their current hideout. Clay didn't like that either. If something went wrong, they wouldn't have any backup nearby. The whole situation didn't sit right with him.

"Haven't encountered any Radicals lately," Reagan said, looking around. She wasn't speaking to anyone in particular, but it was obvious she was reading his mind.

"Helena cut off the leader's head," Bossman said. "All of his little minions are scattering around aimlessly."

"I'm not really sure if that's a good or bad thing," Razor said.

"For now, it should buy us some peace," Bossman sighed.

The group fell silent as they moved deeper into the wooded area. Clay hoped they would find the vehicles soon so he could quickly get out of Bossman's sight. This was incredibly frustrating. Now, he truly understood Jade's brawling session with Bossman when they returned. Clay had to admire Jade's strength even more. He had only been around Bossman for a few hours, and he already wanted to fight him. Jade had to endure days with him.

It took them another 30 minutes before they discovered a small clearing. There were two vehicles there: an SUV and a sedan.

"Here we are," Bossman announced as he approached the SUV.

"Do they have gas?" Reagan asked, with a slight hint of annoyance in her tone, as if she expected the answer to be no.

"Enough to get us back to the hideout."

"Did you have foresight about that, too?"

Bossman chuckled as he opened the SUV door.

"You two check out the sedan," Razor said as he joined Bossman.

Clay approached the sedan and opened the driver's door. It was a habit, but he glanced around for the keys. Reagan walked over and leaned against the door.

"Anything?" she asked him.

"No," Clay said as he finished searching the car. "I don't see the key."

"We don't know how to hotwire a car," Reagan announced.

"I told you we should've brought the little one," Bossman chuckled to Razor.

"No," Razor's voice sounded distant. Clay noticed he was in the driver's seat of the SUV, fiddling with the wires beneath the steering wheel. "I'll do it."

Just then, the SUV roared to life. Razor walked over to the sedan, and Clay quickly stepped out. Razor began working on the car.

"At least the little one would give me more conversation," Bossman sighed. "Unlike Jade's new boy toy."

"Ignore him," Razor mumbled to Clay.

"Oh, come off it!" Bossman shouted. "There's no need for all the secrecy. It's obvious you're the new fuck toy."

"Is that a problem?" Reagan asked as she stood in front of Clay. She nocked an arrow onto the bow she borrowed from Jade.

Bossman chuckled. "Jade can fuck whoever she likes. That doesn't bother me."

The sedan started. Razor quickly got out and pushed Clay into the driver's seat. Reagan walked around to the passenger side, her aim on Bossman, and got in.

"Go back to the hideout," Razor ordered.

Clay shifted the car into drive.

"Just as long as you understand, boy toy," Bossman said before Clay drove off. "In the end, it'll be just me and Jade."

Clay didn't say anything. He kept his eyes locked on Bossman as he drove off. The warning should've frightened him, but it didn't. Bossman might believe it'd just be the two of them, but Clay knew better. He would be there because he didn't plan on ever leaving Jade's side.

~16~

Razor

The hot wind blew onto Razor's face as he and Nick drove to a stash location that Nick knew about. It was a stash spot he had set up. Apparently, before Nick figured out where the Black Coats' HQ was, he created several stash points for supplies. There were three he had made, and they planned to retrieve supplies from them.

Razor rode quietly in the passenger seat, worried about the consequences of Jade's relationship with Clay. He didn't want Nick to obsess over them and risk jeopardizing the mission. Everyone needed to stay focused on finishing this. They had to bring everything to an end. He couldn't bring a child into this chaotic cycle; he had to work toward making it a better world.

"There's a grumpy Razor in my midst," Nick sighed.

"We need to stay focused," Razor kept his eyes on the window.

"Who says I'm not?"

"Jade and Clay, leave them be."

"Oh, Razor," Nick sighed again.

"I'm serious, Nick. Now's not the time for your bullshit."

"But I love her, Razor."

"No, you don't!" Razor looked at him. "You're just playing your little mind games as usual. The shit stops now. Leave my sister alone! You've done enough to her!"

The rage was threatening to burst out of him. Razor was at his breaking point with Nick's presence, just like everyone else. There was a time when he loved Nick and considered him his closest and only friend. But all of that changed when he met Helena. Razor could no longer tolerate Nick's usual antics.

"My, how I missed that rage of yours," Nick chuckled.

"I mean it, Nick."

"Believe it or not, I do love Jade," Nick said, focusing on the road ahead. "But I'm not so delusional to think I actually have a shot with her. I never did. But I'm not the type to give up easily. So, yes, I obsess over her. And I will until the day I die."

"Yeah, well, that might be soon if you keep fucking with her," Razor grumbled.

Nick laughed. "Then I might back off just a little."

Razor sighed. He knew it wasn't guaranteed, but that statement helped him relax a bit. He made his intentions clear. Hopefully, Nick would follow through, even if just for a little while.

They reached the first stash spot, an old, dilapidated shack. A false floor section in the back concealed a few boxes of supplies Nick had hidden there. Razor and Nick quickly loaded the boxes into the SUV and drove away.

"Glad it was still there," Razor said. They needed all the supplies they could get.

"Shocking, really," Nick appeared lost in thought.

Razor thought about Reagan's mention of gas. He glanced at the fuel level gauge. It didn't look like there was much in the tank.

"Is there any gas at the other locations?" he asked.

"We'll be fine, trust me. The other locations aren't too far from here."

"Sure," Razor genuinely wanted to convey that he didn't want to be stranded on the side of the road somewhere. But at this point, it was no use.

They arrived at the second location shortly after. It was an old house. Nick got out and went into the backyard. Razor was slow to follow. He initially thought they would go inside. Nick was at the far corner of the backyard when he picked up a shovel and started digging. He had been digging for about five minutes before he called out to Razor.

"I could use a hand."

Razor walked over and looked down into the freshly dug hole. A few boxes were inside. He grabbed two and headed back to the SUV. Nick was right behind him. Razor loaded the supplies and climbed into the driver's seat. They were quickly on their way again. Maybe they had enough gas to make it back.

The last spot was in a nearby wooded area. Razor followed Nick as he walked along a confusing path until they reached the secret location. A makeshift smugglers' hatch was hidden behind some bushes. This time, Nick pulled out a few bags instead of boxes.

Razor was loading the bags into the SUV when a small group

approached them. He quickly slammed the trunk.

"I hope our tax is in there," a woman said, nodding toward the supplies in the trunk.

"You hoped wrong," Razor said, brushing past her.

"That's how it works around here," a man accompanying the woman said. The other two guys nodded.

"It used to," Nick said as he came up behind him. "Not anymore. And honestly, I don't give a shit about a tax either way."

"I'll let you handle this, Nick," Razor said as he headed to the passenger door.

Nick was already attacking two men before Razor was closing the door. The woman and the other man lingered, unsure if they wanted to attack. They retreated once their comrades hit the ground, but Nick was on them before they could get far. It was like watching a horror movie—a monster or a wild animal unleashed and wreaking havoc on everyone nearby. That's how someone would describe Nick and his presence.

With blood still on his hands, Nick got into the SUV and drove away. Razor sighed. He hoped Nick's riled-up energy would die down before they returned to the hideout.

"Looks like there are still some Radicals around," Razor said.

"Looks like it," Nick said enthusiastically. "They'll be fun to kill."

Razor saw it as a silver lining. If Nick's attention were on the Radicals, then it wouldn't be on Jade. At this moment, Razor would accept any small victories he could get.

~17~

Helena

"Are you sure you know what you're doing?" Helena asked nervously.

"I'm sure," Sunday snapped. "Now hold still, or you'll make me mess up!"

Helena sighed. How did she end up in this situation? She was sitting between Sunday's legs as Sunday began to cut her hair. A nine-year-old shouldn't be allowed near her with scissors, but here she was. Helena was trying to do her usual hair trim, but was struggling. Between feeling nauseous and worrying about Razor's absence, she had a hard time keeping her hands steady. Sunday came over and told her she could help. Helena hesitated at first, but Sunday's insistence on helping finally wore her down.

There was no one else there to help her. Clay and Reagan had come back, minus Razor and Bossman, and Clay quickly took Jade somewhere to talk. Reagan told Helena that Razor and Bossman had gone to retrieve supplies that Bossman had hidden around the area, but that was all. She stayed nearby but did not offer Helena any help with her hair. Yoko and Tatianna were helping Cole and the others go through the supplies they had gathered. So, Sunday was the only one she had.

"At least you're not as squirmy as Jade," Sunday said. Helena could hear the sound of the scissors pick up speed.

"That's because Jade never likes getting her hair done," Helena said. She could only imagine what Sunday had to go through.

"She was terrible," Sunday groaned. "It was like dealing with a big baby."

Helena smiled. "I told her just to cut her hair."

"Same, but she refuses."

Helena laughed a little.

"I will have to pin her down and refresh her hair soon."

"Good luck with that," Helana laughed. She hoped it wouldn't mess up Sunday.

"I think I'll ask that Clay guy to help me keep her still," Sunday said.

"That actually might be a good idea," Helena wished she had thought of that every time she fought with Jade to do her hair. They remained silent for a moment. Sunday seemed very skilled with the scissors. "How do you know how to do all of this?"

"I used to do it with Vivian and the gang," Sunday shrugged. "I used to help cut the guys and girls' hair. Vivian used to say I had a knack for picking things up quickly."

"Oh," Helena wanted to ask her more about them, but Sunday seemed very reluctant to talk about them any further.

"He could've sent a message, you know!" Sunday snapped. "What was he thinking, going on an extra mission?!" Sunday looked over at Reagan. "He didn't leave you a message for Helena?!"

Reagan seemed surprised by Sunday's outburst. She shook her head.

"I am going to give him hell when he gets back," Sunday grumbled.

"It's ok, Sunday."

"No, it's not," Sunday snapped. "You're worried about him. Razor should know better."

Helena had to hold back her laugh. Sunday was a bit of a firecracker. It was clear she was close to Jade, but there was something different about her relationship with Razor. It was as if she were overly protective of him. And it seemed as if Razor was afraid of her. The whole situation was quite comical, actually. Right now, Helena was thankful for Sunday. She was keeping Helena distracted from Razor's ongoing absence.

Brice and his team entered, carrying more supplies and loading them in. Helena watched the door, wondering if Razor would walk in with them. She sighed in disappointment when he didn't.

"We have two vans," Brice announced. "The third one didn't start. I'm not sure what's wrong with it."

"Is it far?" Keeper asked. "I can take a look at it."

"It's not far at all," Brice said.

"I'll go with you," Tatianna said.

"Me too," Reagan said. "Let my brother know when you see him," she said, looking at Helena and Sunday.

"Ok," Sunday said as she examined Helena's hair closely.

"Be safe," Helena said. She noticed that Reagan had been unusually quiet lately. Granted, Reagan was never a big talker to begin with, but she seemed even more silent. Helena wondered if it was because she was grieving for Danita. The two of them had been close to each other. You usually couldn't find one without the other. It was hard losing another group member. Helena might not have been that acquainted with Danita, but she still missed seeing her and hearing her voice.

"So," Sunday said as she ran her fingers through Helena's hair. "What are you hoping for? Boy or girl?"

Helena sighed. "I don't know. I'm still trying to wrap my head around becoming a mother."

"You seem motherly," Sunday handed Helena a hand mirror. "How's this?"

Helena gazed at her reflection in the mirror. She seemed stressed. There were bags under her eyes, and her face appeared shallow. When did she start looking like this? She looked away and focused on her hair. Sunday was doing a good job. Helena was impressed.

"Just a little more off the top, please," Helena said, handing the mirror back to Sunday.

"You got it."

"What about me seems motherly to you?" Sunday, calling Helena motherly, caught her off guard. Helena was so fearful and codependent. Nothing about that seemed motherly to her.

Sunday remained silent for a while. Only the sound of the scissors broke the silence between them.

"Not really sure," Sunday said after a moment. "There's just this vibe you have, that's all."

"I think Jade would be a better mother," Helena admitted.

Sunday snorted. "Jade would be a mother from hell. She's too scary."

Helena smiled, unsure why, but feeling comforted by that statement. "Does she scare you?"

"Constantly, especially when it comes to Bossman."

"She has good reasons for that."

"I know, but that doesn't make her outbursts any less frightening."

"Touché."

"And to think," Sunday sighed. "She used to be my hero."

"Used to be?"

"Well, she still is, but I have a new one too."

"Oh yeah, who?"

"You."

"Me?" Helena was surprised. "How can it be me? You just met me."

Sunday shrugged. "You don't hear the way he talks about you. Anyone who can get Razor to talk like that must be something."

Just then, Razor walked in. For some reason, it felt like he had been gone from her forever. But he was safe and looked unharmed. Helena was more than grateful for that. Sunday quickly got up, handed Helena the mirror again, and went straight over to Razor.

"Took you long enough!" Sunday yelled as she punched Razor in the gut.

"What the hell is your problem?!" He grabbed Sunday by the wrist. Razor looked confused as he furrowed his brow at her. Helena could tell that he was unsure whether to be furious or sympathetic toward her reaction.

"I knew you were an asshole, but not this much of an asshole!"

"I told you to watch your mouth!"

"How could you go on another mission without sending a message to Helena?!" Her voice cracked. "We were worried sick about you! That's not something you do to your pregnant wife! That's not something you do to me," her voice dropped on that last part.

Razor knelt and took Sunday by the chin. "I told you, I will always come back to you and Helena."

"You can't promise that," Sunday cried. Razor quickly wrapped his arms around her and whispered words of comfort.

Helena was overwhelmed by what she saw. Everyone else nearby was a little stunned and confused by the fight. Sunday's emotions were hard to read, and everyone was still getting to know her. But this sight made Helena's heart ache. She knew that Sunday had become close to Razor, but she didn't expect it to be like this. It seemed like she found comfort and safety in him. Helena could understand that feeling.

Helena finally looked in the mirror. Her hair looked perfect. "You did a fantastic job, Sunday. Thank you."

Sunday's face lit up as she wiped away her tears. "Really?" For the first time, Sunday actually looked like a kid to Helena.

"Yes, I'm so glad I found a great hair stylist," Helena smiled.

Razor picked up Sunday and walked over to Helena. He leaned down and kissed her. Sunday rested her head on his shoulder.

"Sorry for taking so long," he said.

"It's ok," Helena smiled. She was just happy that he came back to her safely. "I had Sunday here to watch me."

"She'll get the job done," he smiled as he kissed Sunday's forehead.

Sunday frowned as she tried to wiggle free from his hold. Razor set her on her feet and laughed.

"Done pouting now?" he asked, patting her head.

"Shut up," she said, slapping his hand away.

"Did you get everything you needed?" Helena asked.

"Yeah, we've got everything."

"Not saying I want to see him, but where's Bossman?" Helena thought he'd be with Razor.

"Out Radical hunting."

"Huh?" Helena frowned.

"We need to head out soon," he said. "Otherwise, we'll be compromised."

Sunday punched him in the gut again. "And this is why you don't go out on extra missions!"

~18~

Jade

This *had to end.* That's all Jade could think about as she loaded the van that Yoko and Jackson were driving. She felt bad for Yoko. She would have to endure Jackson and his unpleasant behavior the whole way to Lansing. According to Helena, he had become quite a handful—though Jade couldn't really blame him. Who wouldn't feel angry and resentful after everything? Still, his attitude wasn't exactly pleasant to be around. Cole promised he'd work harder to bring Jackson around. Jade hoped he'd succeed.

They had a total of five vehicles—the DC truck, which they used to travel to Toronto. The SUV and sedan Bossman found. And the two minivans Brice brought back. He initially found three minivans, but Keeper couldn't fix the third one. Either way, it was enough for all of them to travel back to Michigan.

They divided into groups. Yoko and Jackson rode in a minivan packed with supplies. Brice and some members of the Black Coats took the SUV. The remaining members and supplies were in the DC truck. Razor, Helena, Sunday, Cole, Zara, and Bossman rode in the second minivan. Jade, Clay, Reagan, Keeper, and Tatianna were in the sedan. Jade wasn't happy about Sunday riding with Bossman, but Razor and Helena were there, so it gave her some comfort. Besides, she had plenty of other things to worry about.

One of her main worries was Bossman's hidden threat to Clay. Jade didn't question how he knew she was close to Clay. By now, she was sure that Bossman just seemed to sense things. She hated the fact that they would have to keep looking over their shoulders.

"He's not stupid enough to make a move," Clay told her. He had just returned from the supply run with Razor and Bossman. He took her back to his room to talk about what had happened.

"You can't be sure," Jade said. How could he stay so calm about all this?

"He needs you, Jade. It would be stupid of him to get on your bad side even further."

Jade had to give it to him there. That would be an idiotic move on Bossman's part. And he wasn't known for being stupid.

Jade sighed. "You're right."

"Let's just focus on the mission, and then we'll come up with a plan to kill him."

"How do you just get me?" Jade had walked into his arms. Clay wrapped his arms tightly around her and kissed the top of her head.

"You're pretty easy to read," he said softly, his voice low and gentle, as he pressed his lips to her hair.

Jade smiled. She didn't expect to have a moment like this ever again, so she took a moment to cherish it.

"I think that's all that can fit in here," Yoko sighed as she placed a box in the last available space in the van.

Jade nodded, focusing on their current situation. They were leaving in the morning. When Razor returned from his extra mission with Bossman, he told everyone that there were still Radicals lurking around. Bossman went out to "hunt" them, but it was time for them all to leave and head back to Michigan as soon as possible. The whole scenario didn't sit right with Jade, but she was ready to go.

Mostly, she was just ready to end all of this—the constant running and fighting, the constant fear and paranoia, the constant terror. Jade just wanted peace. It's what they all deserved: *peace.* But could that happen for them? Did they deserve it? After all, they were all murderers, weren't they? Jade was one of the biggest of them all. However, she was sure that Bossman and Razor had her beat. But still, the question remained—did they deserve peace? For the sake of the future, they did. For the sake of her unborn niece or nephew, they needed it. There were no ifs, ands, or buts about it. Everything had to end.

But Jade wondered how it would all end for her. Deep down, she knew it wouldn't be peaceful. Still, that didn't bother her.

"Ready to go?" Yoko asked as she shut the van's door.

Jade nodded. "Let's finish this."

~19~

Jade

It seemed that fear and rage had been the only emotions consuming Jade lately. She couldn't stop tapping the blade of her knife against her thigh as the group set up camp for the night. They were at Danford Island Park in Dimondale, Michigan. Jade wasn't sure why they picked a park to settle in, but there they were. The trip lasted half the day. Jade was sure it would have been faster during normal times, but they still arrived there quicker than she expected. They still weren't in Lansing yet, but Bossman thought it was better for them to raid some sweeps before heading to Lansing.

"Is there any scheduled soon?" Razor asked as he began to start a fire.

"There should be," Bossman shrugged. "I'll do a little reconnaissance later tonight."

Jade stopped her fidgeting. "Hey, don't bring any unnecessary heat on us."

Bossman laughed. "I think it's a little too late for that, my sweet Jade."

Jade rolled her eyes. He had a point. She couldn't shake her uneasiness. There was something about being back in Michigan that made her anxious. This was the source of her pain and fear. She didn't have that feeling when she was in New York. After their escape from Junior, they hadn't run into a DC officer. She wasn't sure why, but New York didn't scare her. Michigan was a completely different story.

Now she was back here. Now she would have to face the DCs again. Sure, she could fight them without any trouble, but it still scared her for some reason.

"Should we figure out shifts?" Clay asked.

"Let's do it," Razor said.

"I'll take first watch," Jade said quickly. There was no way she'd be sleeping anytime soon.

"So will I," Bossman sighed. "That way, I can go off later."

"I'll take it too, then," Clay said.

"No," Jade said, looking at him. He frowned. "It'll be fine."

"Alright then," Razor said. "Who'll be next?"

While everyone else was signing up for their spots as lookouts, Jade approached Helena and Sunday, who were setting up their sleeping area. Jade noticed how close Sunday was getting to Helena. It reassured her to see they were looking out for each other.

"Hey," Jade greeted them as Sunday was carrying a sleeping bag into a tent they'd set up. "How are you feeling, Helena?"

"A mix of starving and feeling nauseous."

Jade frowned. "Sorry."

"Really, did they have to pick a hard ground for you to sleep on?" Sunday snapped as she walked out of the tent. She went over to the nearby pile of supplies, looking for more blankets. "How are you supposed to sleep on a hard surface?"

Helena laughed. "I'll be fine, Mom."

"You need your rest," Sunday said as she grabbed a blanket and some clothing. "You couldn't really sleep in the van because of that asshat yapping."

Jade glanced at Helena, confused.

"She means Bossman," Helena's laugh grew louder. "I think he kept at it just to annoy her."

"He's just rude!" Sunday complained as she stomped back into the tent. "I told him you needed to sleep. Even the doc agreed with me!"

"My ears are burning," Bossman shouted.

"I'm talking about you, you ass-for-brains!" Sunday stormed out of the tent. "I wasn't hiding it!"

Bossman laughed. "You are a raging thing, little one."

"And you're such an inconsiderate fuck!"

"Such big and vulgar language," he shook his head as if he were disappointed.

"I don't care what you think!" Sunday said as she walked over to Helena and took her hand.

"Don't get her worked up," Razor sighed.

"You know," Bossman said as he walked toward her, "The more you shout and curse, the more afraid you seem. Stop trying to act tough, little one."

"Go find a tree trunk to screw!" Sunday frowned. "No one here is afraid of you!"

Bossman chuckled. "Is that right?" Bossman was moving closer to her.

Sunday's body trembled, but she refused to back down. She stepped in front of Helena as if to protect her, her shaking hand reaching for her knife's handle. Before Jade could move to step in, Razor blocked Bossman's path.

"Leave. Her. Alone." Almost every vein in Razor's body was bulging—the sight kind of frightened Jade.

Bossman chuckled as he raised his hands. "Apologies, my friend. But that little one has a sharp tongue. It's hard to remember that she's just a kid."

Cole cleared his throat. "Helena, I have some extra pillows for you," he said, walking over to them.

"Thanks, Cole," Helena said, a bit flustered from Sunday's sudden confrontation with Bossman. "Sunday, can you grab them for me?"

Sunday quietly grabbed the pillows from Cole and entered the tent. Jade watched her, noticing that Sunday looked defeated.

"She certainly is a lively one," Cole chuckled.

"She has to play tough," Jade said as she watched Sunday make up Helena's sleeping pallet. "There's no other way to be in this world."

"Well, she'll definitely come in handy," Cole smiled at them. "I'm going to see what's on the menu for dinner."

"Something good, I hope," Jade sighed.

"I just hope I can keep it down," Helena muttered.

"Helena, I'll make something that can help you with that."

"Thanks, Cole."

"Get some rest," Cole said as he walked over to talk to Keeper in his sleeping area.

Sunday arrived at the entrance of the tent. "It's ready, Helena."

Helena motioned for Jade to join her. Jade followed her inside the tent. Sunday made a sleeping pallet that occupied most of the space in the tent.

Jade understood why she arranged it that way. She could make the pallet more comfortable by adding all the covers to it. Helena took off her shoes and sat on the pallet.

"This is perfect, Sunday," she sighed as she propped herself up on the pillows.

"Thank you," Sunday mumbled, her eyes fixed on the ground.

"Take off your shoes, and come here," Helena ordered, opening her arms.

Sunday obeyed and quickly snuggled into Helena's arms. She rested her head on Helena's chest, and Helena kissed her forehead.

"You need to be careful about what you say," Helena said softly. "And how you say it."

"I won't let anyone bully me," Sunday whispered, wiping away her tears.

"I know, my little firecracker," Helena laughed. "But I need you to be safe."

Jade's heart swelled in the moment. Helena looked like a natural—her mother instincts on full display. Jade couldn't be prouder of her sister and was so thankful to Sunday. They were perfect for each other.

"Some people would want to 'punish' you for the way you speak to them," Jade added. "You have to watch out for that."

"I just want to show them I'm not afraid," Sunday's voice cracked.

"You demonstrate that through your fighting," Jade said. "I know you can do it."

"But I don't want it to come to that," Sunday cried harder. "I figure if I talk tough, they will think twice about messing with me."

"That won't always be the case. You're gonna have to fight," Jade hated telling her that, but it was the truth.

"I don't like fighting, Jade."

"That's the way of the world."

"It's best just to try to avoid the encounter altogether," Helena comforted Sunday as she shot Jade a stern look.

Crap. She was in trouble.

Luckily for Jade, Razor walked in and took in the scene. "Everyone ok?"

"We're getting there," Helena said as Sunday wiped away more tears and buried her head in Helena's shoulder.

"Let's just keep it cool for the rest of the night," his voice pleaded.

"I'm sorry, Razor." Sunday's voice was muffled because she kept her face buried into Helena's shoulder.

"It's ok. Just be careful from now on," he looked at Jade. "Your time to keep watch is after everyone is finished eating dinner."

Jade nodded, and Razor quickly left.

**

Dinner was uneventful. Jade ate her meal with Helena and Sunday in their tent. Clay popped in to check on them and then joined his sister for their meal. Helena had no trouble eating her food; the problem was keeping it down. Cole came in and gave her something to help. A few minutes later, she drifted off to sleep. Sunday quickly followed. Helena held her tight in her arms as they slept. Jade smiled and quietly left the tent to prepare for her watch.

Jade went to Clay's tent, located near the back of the camp, by Cole and Zara. He was sitting on his sleeping pallet when she entered.

"Hey," she said as she looked into her bags sitting in the back corner of the tent. She wanted to have a few more knives with her.

"Preparing to take watch?" he asked, looking worried.

"Yeah. Hopefully, it'll be an uneventful time," she said, adding a few more knives to the knife holster belt that Keeper made her. It could hold multiple knives, which she loved.

"I hope so," he paused. "Try not to bring up that incident with Sunday."

Jade sighed. She was trying to forget it. She was glad Razor stepped in, but she was disappointed she didn't intervene sooner. Maybe she was unknowingly growing comfortable around Bossman. The thought made her furious. That wasn't it. It was this stupid mission. She had to be diplomatic and let things go, all because of the mission. This whole situation was becoming more annoying.

"Understood," she finally said. She didn't like it, but she could see where Clay was coming from. And she didn't want to make him worry.

"Thank you," he said, taking off his shoes. "I'm going to try to get some shut-eye."

Jade noticed his emphasis on the word "try." She walked over to him, kneeled beside him, and kissed him. "I'll be ok," she said as she pulled back and looked him in the eyes.

Clay smiled. "I'm here if you need me."

Jade nodded, stood up, and left the tent. She headed to the front of the camp. Nearly everyone was inside their tents, with a few stragglers still getting their sleeping areas ready. Jade nodded to them as she passed.

Bossman was sitting on a log up front. Jade sighed when she saw him. How was this going to go? She planned to ignore him, but sometimes her emotions got the better of her, especially when it came to him.

Jade walked past him and leaned against a tree across from him. She definitely wasn't planning to sit next to him on the log.

"Oh, good," he said, fiddling with a knife. "I was beginning to think you wouldn't show."

Jade rolled her eyes. "I wasn't gonna ditch my shift because of you."

"That's good to know."

Jade didn't say anything. She shook her head and looked around. She didn't notice anything unusual—nor did she hear anything. Everything seemed fine. Soon, they'd need to go out and walk the perimeter. Jade preferred to do that alone.

"Pissy with me?" Bossman suddenly asked.

Jade looked at him for a second. "You're kidding, right?"

"I'm not talking about that," he sighed. "I'm talking about what happened with the little one."

"What happened with you and Sunday was to be expected," she said. "Not even children are safe from you."

"I'm sorry," he paused. "For everything."

"Too late to grow a conscience now." Jade hated this. He was not supposed to feel remorseful. He was supposed to be evil—pure evil. And Jade wouldn't see it any other way.

"You know, growing up..." he began.

"I don't want to hear about your sad, pathetic childhood!" Jade snapped. "Nothing you say can undo all the harm you've caused. You're a monster, plain and simple."

"And I guess you're just so innocent?" he countered. Jade could hear a hint of anger in his tone. "It's not like your hands are completely blood-free, Jade. Or did you forget that was why I loved you in the first place?"

"I never claimed to be innocent," Jade shot back heatedly. "And did *you* forget that you created an environment where killing was necessary?!"

"I'm trying to make this right," Bossman sighed. His voice sounded sincere.

"The only way you can do that is by dying," Jade said. "The world would be better for it."

"Some might say the same about you, Jade."

"As long as I get to kill you first, I'm good with that," Jade said, and she meant it.

~20~

Jade

Sunlight blinded Jade as she woke up. Clay was slowly moving his arms away from her. She managed to fall asleep quickly after her shift as a lookout. Bossman had walked off, saying he was going to do some recon on the area. Jade didn't care. They didn't talk much during their shift, which she appreciated. There wasn't much more to say after they both admitted that the world would be better off without them.

Jade groaned as she got up. Clay was asleep when she returned. There was one moment during the night when she rolled over and found him gone. She knew he had left to do his shift with Reagan, but she didn't hear him when he came back.

Jade stretched as she tried to hold back a yawn. Clay was still sleeping, and she didn't want to wake him.

"Jade," Sunday whispered outside her tent.

"Hmm."

"Um, would you take watch with me?"

"Watch?" Jade frowned. Surely, Razor disapproved of this.

"Yeah, um, Razor and that Jackson guy just finished," she whispered nervously. "I asked Razor if I could keep watch while everyone else was sleeping. And he said only if you'd do it with me."

Jade sighed. *Great.* Razor was trying to make her the bad guy. But Jade was in no mood to argue with Sunday. They could keep watch for an hour or so. That should satisfy Sunday enough.

"Give me five minutes," Jade yawned.

"Ok, thanks," Sunday whispered. Jade could tell she was relieved by her response. It seemed like she expected Jade to say no.

Jade grabbed a water bottle and her toothbrush, both of which were sitting on a small, folding table near the front of the tent. She brushed her teeth, washed her face, and then put a couple of knives into her thigh strap before heading over to Clay.

"Going to keep watch with Sunday," she whispered to him before kissing him on the cheek.

Clay chuckled. "Have fun."

"I'll try," Jade sighed.

Clay chuckled as she walked away.

Sunday was looking up at the sky when Jade stepped out. She was frowning deeply, as if something was bothering her. Jade zipped up the tent.

"You think a storm is coming?" Sunday asked.

Jade looked up at the sky as she stood. Everything seemed normal enough. "It's hard to tell."

"I noticed we haven't been getting many natural disasters lately," Sunday said, walking toward the front of camp.

"Don't jinx us," Jade hissed as she followed. But Sunday was right. There hadn't been many strange natural disasters lately. The last one was the earthquake that happened at the Real Canadian Superstore, and that seemed so long ago—a few months, at least. An uncommon natural disaster never stayed quiet for that long. That knowledge made Jade uneasy.

"Not sure if that's a good or bad thing," Sunday said.

"We'll just have to stay prepared," Jade sighed, as if there weren't already enough things for her to worry about.

When they reached the front, Sunday quickly sat down on the log. Jade sat beside her. She looked around for a moment. Nothing appeared unusual. She then glanced at Sunday, who was frowning at the view before her.

"How's Helena?" Jade asked.

"She seemed fine when I left her," Sunday looked around. "She slept through the night."

"Take out your knife," Jade said. Sunday looked at her, confused. "You need to sharpen it." Jade pulled out her sharpening stone. She took out one of her knives and demonstrated how to sharpen it. She then passed it over to Sunday to give it a try.

Sunday concentrated on repeating what Jade showed her. Jade watched her for a moment.

"You're not being a bother to Razor and Helena, are you?" Jade asked after a while.

"No," Sunday kept her eyes on the knife and the sharpening stone. "I'm just trying to help them."

"Good," Jade said. "I need you to help them as much as you can."

Sunday nodded.

"You can stop. That should be good enough," Jade took the sharpening stone as Sunday sheathed her knife. "You want to make sure your knife stays sharp."

Sunday nodded. Jade noticed she looked uncomfortable. "Um, we should start gathering baby supplies. I imagine they're hard to come by."

Jade frowned. "Good point."

"Should I bring it up with Razor?"

"Maybe Keeper," Jade said. "He can make whatever he can't find."

"For some things, yes. But what about baby formula? We'll need that if Helena can't produce enough milk."

"How do you know that?"

"That's how we lost my little brother," Sunday said, looking down. "He ended up starving to death because we had a hard time finding substance for him."

"I'm so sorry, Sunday." There was so much Jade didn't know about Sunday. It was hard for her to open up about certain things.

"Maybe I should ask the doc about that," Sunday suggested as she looked at Jade.

"That's a good idea."

Sunday smiled. Jade was happy that Sunday wanted to be useful. And it was a huge relief for her. They sat quietly for a moment. Sunday kept scanning the area intently, as if she were expecting someone to attack at any moment. Jade almost laughed. Then Sunday suddenly stiffened. Jade turned around and saw Bossman walking toward them.

"On another shift so soon?" he asked as he approached.

"You look like shit," Jade said, looking him up and down. He looked tired.

Bossman shrugged and looked at Sunday. "I'm sorry for my behavior yesterday, little one."

"I don't care," Sunday said, rolling her eyes.

"Fair enough," he sighed.

"Find anything?" Jade asked.

"I did. I'll elaborate in an hour or so. I'm going to get some rest in the DC truck. Make sure no one tries to kill me in the meantime," he said, walking off toward the vehicles.

"Can't make any promises," Jade said.

Bossman laughed as he walked away.

"Will I be at the raids?" Sunday asked once Bossman was out of sight.

"Do you want to be?"

"Yes, please," Sunday said with a smile.

"We'll see where Razor wants to place you."

"I'm not stupid, you know," Sunday frowned at her. "I know you and Razor make comments like that to force the other one to be the bad guy. If you don't want me to do it, then say so."

"You're a child, Sunday."

"But I want to be useful."

"You hate fighting, remember?"

"You just told me that I have to!" Sunday snapped. She had Jade there.

"We'll see what Razor says," Jade said.

"Whatever," Sunday grumbled.

"Ah, good morning, ladies," Cole greeted as he approached. "I was looking for you, Sunday."

"Why?"

"I'd like to teach you a few things that will help me when taking care of Helena."

"Really?" Sunday's mood lightened up.

"Oh, yes. You'll be a big help."

Sunday looked at Jade as if she were asking for permission.

"Go ahead," Jade encouraged. "I'll be ok by myself."

"Thank you," Sunday said, jumping up from the log.

"Oh, Bossman wants to update us in an hour," Jade said.

"I'll relay the message," Cole said before walking away.

**

An hour later, they all sat around a campfire as breakfast was being passed out. Oatmeal was on the menu, and Jade was glad. She sat between Clay and Jackson. Bossman was seated directly across from her, next to Zara and Cole. Jackson had his back to the group, not wanting to look at Bossman. Jade couldn't blame him. Razor, Helena, and Sunday were sitting further down from Jade.

"What did you find?" Razor asked once everyone was seated with a bowl of oatmeal.

"Their schedules," Bossman said between bites. "One is tomorrow morning. It's just about two miles from here."

"Anything else?" Razor pressed.

"Chase knows we've escaped from Junior. It appears he's assembled a team to head to Toronto. He's with them this time."

"Is that wise?" Helena asked. "For the President to go off like that? Wouldn't that raise flags?"

"It would, Helena. But there's so much going on right now," Bossman said as he set his now empty bowl down. "Apparently, there have been major protests from the people since our encounter on the Detroit River." The group all looked around at each other, confused. This was news to them. This was definitely news to Jade. People were protesting?

"You're shitting us, right?" Yoko asked.

"In the major cities, yes," Bossman said. "It's been big in Detroit and Lansing. But it's happening all around the country."

"Protests from debtors?" Jade asked. For some reason, she just couldn't understand it.

"Debtors, providers, and even some Congress members... at least, that's what my intel says."

"So, these prison breaks might actually be the key to overthrowing Chase," Razor said.

"Absolutely."

"Well, we need to prioritize getting people first," Jade said.

"Right," Razor sighed. "About that, where will you be, Nick? Surely, you know it's a bad idea for you to be there."

"I'll be gathering more intel," Bossman said. "I need to narrow down which prisons I want to hit and their schematics."

"Sounds good."

"Where are we going to put all these people?" Tatianna asked. "It'll look too suspicious with so many people."

"I know a place," Jackson grumbled, his back still turned to the group.

"Where?" Jade asked as she looked over at him.

"I'll show you."

"Alright, I think we're good then," Razor said, standing. "I'll go with Jade and Jackson. Clay, Cole, Zara, and Brice, you all come up with a plan for the sweep tomorrow."

Jade got up and followed Jackson, with Razor right behind her. The rest of the group started cleaning up or heading back to their tents. Jade thought Sunday would ask to come along, but she didn't. She figured Sunday wanted to stay with Helena more.

They followed Jackson quietly for a moment. Once they exited the park, they turned right onto Washington Street. They walked a block and then took a left onto Bridge Street. Jackson stopped in front of a row of businesses. He pointed to a store that used to be a café and bakery.

"We can begin with this building and then expand to the next," he stated.

Jade looked at the buildings. They all had an upstairs space that could hold more people if needed.

"Are they cleared?" Razor asked.

"Yeah. Keeper, Yoko, and I checked it out."

"Good, we have somewhere to set up," Razor looked at it for a while. Then he turned to Jade and Jackson. "Let's get everyone over here to set up for the night. That way, we're not trying to figure it out tomorrow."

"Alright," Jackson said. For the first time, it sounded like he was satisfied. Jade hoped this signaled a turning point in his behavior.

"It seems like we'll have everything ready for the sweep tomorrow," Jade said.

"Looks like it," Razor said, walking away.

Jade tried to ignore the knots in her stomach as she thought about tomorrow.

~21~

Razor

The plan was straightforward—at least, to Razor. There would be the main fighters, who would distract the DC officers while the debtors escaped, and the guides, who would lead the debtors to the hideout— seemed simple enough. But nothing was ever that easy. The fighters included Razor, Jade, Clay, Reagan, Jackson, Tatianna, Keeper, and Zara. The guides started with Yoko, Brice, and a few Black Coats members, ending with Helena, Sunday, and Cole. At first, Sunday protested about being left behind, but she eventually was content to stay with Helena. Razor was thankful for that.

They all took their positions. Razor and Jade would lead the charge.

Clay and Reagan were high up, taking out the DCs from a distance. The others were on the ground, directing everyone where to go. The whole setup reminded Razor of the first time they started doing this. When they were gathering people to help take down Nick, they were now focused on a different enemy: Chase, the President. It's strange how quickly things changed.

Jade couldn't stop pacing, and it was making Razor edgy. He could sense the nervous energy radiating from her, which was putting him in a bad mood.

"Worried about something?" he asked.

She laughed harshly. "What's not to worry about?"

They were at the corner of a small neighborhood, not too far from their hideout. There was no telling where the DC officers would storm in, but Razor figured this was the best spot to be.

"I really didn't expect to be doing this again," Jade grumbled.

"You spent the entire time in Canada complaining about how you wanted to get back here," Razor said.

"To kill Bossman!" she snapped. "Not to be doing this!"

"What? Helping people?"

"Don't give me that!"

"Get over yourself, Jade." Razor didn't want to argue with her right now. "All of this is much bigger than your bloodlust for Nick."

"Like you didn't do the same thing."

"And look where that got me."

Jade didn't say anything. She just sighed and rolled her eyes. Any other time, Razor would have supported her anger. He'd done it before. But things have changed. His perspective had changed. It had to. He needed to do everything possible to create a better environment for his unborn child. If that meant Jade wouldn't get her way, so be it.

The only flaw in this plan was that they had no way to communicate. So, there was no way for them to know in advance if the DCs were arriving. However, they had an indication: a few blocks away, people started to come out of their houses. A few seconds later, the sounds of trucks rushing down the street could be heard.

"Here we go," Razor said. Jade took off running before he could ask if she was ready. She quickly encountered an officer. Her knife was already going into an officer's neck before he could fully get out of the truck. It was clear that she was taking her anger out on them.

Razor charged into the fight. He saw Jackson, Tatianna, Keeper, and Zara jump in as well. While fending off officers, he had given the debtors directions to Yoko and Brice as they passed by. Surprisingly, they listened to him. He was a wanted man now. The word had officially spread that he was no longer on the opposing side.

"Fucking traitor!" an officer yelled as he charged at Razor.

The officer tried to go for Razor's legs, but Razor had his arms wrapped around the officer's neck and was twisting it before the officer could get a good grip on him. The officer dropped to the ground as another officer made their way to Razor.

Jade was no longer in his sight as he fought off more officers. Tatianna was a few houses ahead of him, fighting and guiding debtors to Yoko and Brice. He started to see arrows flying around, one of which hit the officer who was about to attack him, so he knew he was within Reagan's range. Oddly enough, there weren't many DC officers here. Razor counted seven trucks, each with two officers onboard. That wasn't nearly enough for a neighborhood sweep. Was the number of officers finally dwindling?

There was a big commotion ahead. Razor couldn't get a clear view of what was happening, but he knew it wasn't good. There was a lot of screaming and shouting. A large crowd was gathering a block ahead.

Razor pushed his way to the front, still guiding people to safety as he went. As he moved through the crowd, people were yelling and cursing at something happening in the middle. Finally, he saw it—mob mentality.

The debtors now swarmed the remaining officers. Razor could hear the screams of the officers as they were attacked. It was a sound he would never forget—terrifying. The situation had taken a horrifying turn. The debtors were no longer fleeing; they were attacking. They were fighting back.

"No more hiding!" a man shouted. "No more cowering in the dark! Fight back! Fight back!"

"Fight back! Fight back! Fight back!" the crowd yelled.

Jade stood off to the side, smirking as if she enjoyed the view. At least they wouldn't need to persuade these people to fight and help with the prison breaks. The people were at their breaking point. Razor moved to stand beside Jade. They stood quietly, watching the crowd rebel. Finally, the chaos ceased. The officers were dead. The crowd then turned its attention to him and Jade.

"Join us," Jade said, and the crowd burst into cheers.

They guided the people back to their hideout. It all went easier than expected. Razor wasn't sure where the shift came from, but it seemed a lot had happened during their time in Canada.

**

It only took three buildings to house everyone comfortably. Thanks to Cole and his leadership skills, they managed to calm everyone down and settle into their new quarters quickly.

"I'm happy everything went smoothly," Helena sighed with relief.

"Same," Razor saw Jade leaning against the door to their hideout. She had been avoiding him since the raid. "Heads up, Jade might be pissy with me."

"Great," Helena grumbled.

"I need to go meet Nick," Razor said. "I was going to take Jade, but I don't think that's a good idea anymore."

"Yeah, maybe you should take Clay or Reagan," Helena suggested.

"Agreed," Razor said, looking around for them. "And maybe Cole."

In the end, Razor left with Reagan, Zara, and Cole to meet up with Nick. Nick was still staying in the park, where he planned to remain during the whole operation. Razor was relieved with his decision. He didn't want any of the debtors to see him.

"How'd it go?" Nick asked, sitting around the dead remains of a campfire.

"Smoother than expected," Razor said, sitting across from him. The others sat with him.

"Looks like you were right about the people rebelling," Reagan said. "They did all the heavy lifting for us."

"Is that right?" Nick chuckled.

"The time for this new regime to be overthrown has finally come," Cole sighed. "This moment once seemed unlikely."

"How many officers?" Nick asked Razor.

"About 14."

"For a neighborhood sweep?" Nick shook his head. "There's clearly no one leading them."

"I think they might be here just to keep up appearances," Razor said. "You know the task force is made up of criminalized and egotistical people. Once things start to crumble, they focus on protecting themselves."

"Well, this looks like the perfect time to carry out our plan."

"Which is?" Reagan asked.

"Have I told you how much I like you?" Nick smirked.

"More times than I'd like," Reagan sighed.

Nick chuckled before going on. "There's an unorthodox prison nearby."

"I think I've heard of it," Razor said, frowning as he tried to remember the name.

"Oh no, please don't tell me," Cole sighed.

"That very one, my friend," Nick looked at Reagan and Zara. "It's the Nursing & Rehab Center. In small town areas like this, where larger prisons aren't usually nearby, they often create their own prisons. Usually, it's healthcare facilities."

"Much more convenient to catch and imprison debtors that way," Razor explained. Fortunately, they couldn't do that with all hospitals and health care facilities, though.

"That outside-the-box thinking is why Chase loves Michigan so much," Nick said.

"So, this would be a major blow to him," Zara said.

"Absolutely," Nick said, smiling.

Razor found it strange; he'd never thought he'd be fighting alongside Nick again. But here he was. Hopefully, it wouldn't be on the wrong side of history again.

~22~

Jade

It had been so long since Jade felt hopeful, but that's how she was feeling now—hopeful. When those debtors saw her fighting those DC officers, they didn't hesitate to step in and help. They fought alongside her. They fought back. They no longer wanted to sit back and hide. They no longer wanted to cower. They no longer wanted just to survive. They wanted to thrive. And Jade didn't need to give them a long speech. They were already there, ready to take back control of their lives.

"Ow!" Jade shouted. Her hopeful feeling quickly faded as she sat between Sunday's legs.

"Oh, shut it, you big baby!" Sunday snapped. She was being needlessly rough as she fixed Jade's braids. Jade knew that Sunday was annoyed with her. Jade was still angry with Razor, and Sunday wasn't too fond of that.

"It might help if you weren't so rough!"

"Oh, whatever!"

"If my whining bothers you so much, then stop doing my hair," Jade grumbled.

"So, Helena would have to deal with you?" Sunday said while working on detangling a knot in Jade's hair. "I don't think so."

Jade sighed in frustration. Sunday could be a lot at times. While Jade appreciated her protectiveness over them, it could be overwhelming.

"Ok, *mother*," Jade sneered.

"Ha, ha, ha," Sunday deadpanned. "How long are you going to give Razor the cold shoulder?"

"It's been a day."

"A day too long."

"He will get the cold shoulder for as long as he keeps vouching for Bossman," Jade stated.

"Razor is not vouching for him."

"Oh, because you know so much about this!"

"I know you're acting like a selfish brat!"

"That's rich coming from you!" Jade said, turning to face her. "Weren't you the one ready to pull your knife on him?"

"Because I was defending Helena," Sunday glared. "I make sure it's always about them. You're making this about you."

"Try acting like a kid, Sunday."

"It's funny how you want me to act like a kid when it's convenient for you."

"You will never understand it," Jade said, turning away from Sunday. "He hasn't taken away the people you loved."

"And maybe you should focus more on the ones who are here," Sunday snapped. "Razor and Helena are stressed enough. They don't have time to deal with your tantrums. So get your head out of your shithole."

Jade remained silent because she didn't have a comeback. Sunday had a way with words that sometimes left Jade speechless. They both stayed silent as Sunday finished styling Jade's hair. Once she finished, Jade quickly created some distance from Sunday. It would be a while before she let Sunday do her hair again. If Sunday wanted to pick sides, so be it.

Jade went off to find Clay. She needed new things to talk about. She found him in their makeshift room. They lived on the second floor, next to the old café and bakery. It wasn't as crowded as the place next door. The café seemed to serve as a temporary headquarters for them.

"Someone's grumpy," Clay said as Jade entered.

"Is it that obvious?"

"I told you, you're easy to read," he laughed.

"Well, Sunday wasn't all sunshine and rainbows when she was doing my hair," Jade sighed as she plopped down on their sleeping pallet.

"She never is."

Jade concentrated on removing her boots. "She's pissed at me for how I've been treating Razor."

Clay didn't say anything. He slid his arm around her waist and pulled her close. He kissed her forehead as she rested her head on his chest.

"Do you think I'm wrong for giving him the cold shoulder?" she asked, noticing his silence on the situation.

It took him a while before he spoke. "I think we all need to focus on the task at hand."

"That's a roundabout way to say I'm wrong."

"A lot is happening right now. If we don't stay focused, things could quickly go south. We have too much at stake."

"Point taken," Jade sighed. When it came to her anger, she felt alone. And it hurt because, for the first time, it felt like Razor wasn't on her side.

"Everything will get sorted out eventually," Clay said. "But for now, let's just focus on this prison break."

"Ok," Jade said. Clay was right. All she needed now was to focus on the prison break. It had to succeed. Hopefully, the people there were like the debtors they had just rescued. Everyone would be willing and eager to fight.

**

"Today will be a turning point in history," Cole said to the crowd as they gathered outside the café. He stood on a bench in front so everyone could see him. It was time for the prison break, and Cole wanted to share a few words of encouragement with the people. "Today marks a moment in history where you tell this government, no more!"

A few spectators cheered in the crowd.

"No more being subjected to torture and terror! No more feeling afraid and defeated! No more feeling hopeless and oppressed! The time has come to fight back! Fight back against the powers that be! Fight back against those who are supposed to serve and protect you! Fight back! And keep fighting until your dying breath!

"Fight back! Fight back!"

"Rejoice now, everyone!" Cole continued. "For we will no longer live in the red! We are heading into the black!"

"Into the black! Into the black! Into the black!" the crowd chanted as they marched off. Jade followed, deeply impressed by Cole's speech. She knew he had a way with words, but she had never seen it in action before. This was how he was able to gather a following easily. Luckily, he used his smooth-talking skills for good.

Razor, Helena, and Sunday walked alongside Cole, who was near the front. Jackson, Zara, and Brice followed just behind them. Tatianna, Keeper, and Yoko were in the middle of the crowd. The rest of the Black Coats members were scattered throughout the group. Jade, Clay, and Reagan were bringing up the rear. Jade wanted to stay focused, so she put some distance between herself, Razor, and Helena. That seemed like the best choice for now.

They were roughly three miles from the prison. The crowd fell silent as they approached. According to Bossman's intel, there weren't enough officers left to be stationed around the perimeter of the prison grounds, or more accurately, the nursing and rehabilitation center. Jade couldn't believe the rumors were true. The DCs really did convert old healthcare facilities into prisons. Just when she thought they couldn't be any more evil.

As they approached the grounds, Jade was unsettled by the eerie atmosphere. The area was filled with trees and foliage, making it feel like anything or anyone could emerge at any moment. But to her relief, nothing happened. Jade finally saw the building and its layout as it came into view. Smaller, connected structures surrounded two large L-shaped buildings. The group would need to split up to swarm the facilities.

As they approached the prison's entrance, Jade expected someone to come out and greet them. No one did. Everyone paused, waiting for instructions. Cole glanced at them and smirked.

"Riot," he ordered calmly.

Jade watched with admiration as the group swarmed the building.

~23~

Razor

During his time as a DC officer, Razor had never seen debtors behave like this. Usually, debtors ran from DC officers, but now they were charging at them. Cole only had to say one word, *'riot,'* and that's precisely what they did. The group swarmed the nursing and rehab center so quickly that the officers and guards had no idea what hit them. They were being dragged out of the buildings by angry debtors in less than ten minutes. Razor was stunned—the system's destruction was slowly unfolding.

The first prison break was a complete success. Most of the prisoners were dazed and confused, while others were ecstatic about their freedom.

Cole, Keeper, and a couple of debtors who used to be nurses inspected the prisoners and assisted those in need of medical care. After that, Cole did what he does best: he motivated the people. He urged them to fight. Most of the prisoners agreed to fight, but some just wanted to leave and find a safe place, and Cole told them to do just that.

The momentum was building. The traction was gaining. Razor was confident they could make a difference now. Everything was starting to come together. They could finally change what was happening in this country.

"I didn't realize just how lethal you were, Cole," Nick said as they regrouped at Danford Island Park. Nick was hiding in the dense woods when the prison break happened. He saw everything unfold.

"I think you're overestimating me," Cole chuckled.

"And I think you're downplaying just how cunning you can be."

"Where do we go from here?" Razor asked. He wanted to keep their success going. This time, it was just Nick, Cole, and him meeting. Jade was still ignoring him — which he thought was for the best. Everyone else was busy finding space for the prisoners to settle in.

"Just imagine how far you'd have gone if we left you alone, Cole," Nick continued before turning his attention to Razor. "We spread out. Let the chaos run wild. Raiding the sweeps in Potterville should work."

"That's the next small town over, right?" Razor asked.

"Right. But the size of the town doesn't matter," Nick said.

"It'll still send the right message," Cole agreed. "How long do you think it'll take for the news to reach Chase?"

"A couple of weeks, give or take," Nick smiled. "There's been a lot of turnover in the head position of the DC task force. No one can hack it."

"So, a response to all of this will be slow," Razor nodded.

"And by then, it'll be too late," Cole sighed. "There'll be no turning back. This time, I'll make sure of it."

"I'm getting shivers," Nick said with glee.

"Keep it in your pants, Nick," Razor said. "What area in Potterville should we hit?"

Nick chuckled as he provided them with the location.

"Let's get to work, old friend," Cole said as he and Razor walked away, leaving Nick to his own devices.

"Let's do it."

**

It's incredible what can be achieved in just a few weeks. After their first successful prison break, the group started conducting raids in Potterville. They raided three sweeps there, then returned to Dimondale to regroup before heading over to Holt. There, they conducted a couple of raids and then started planning another prison break.

Oddly enough, it was at another nursing and rehab center. There were five buildings on the grounds. One was the nursing and rehab center, but the other four belonged to a different facility that had been converted. According to the debtors who lived in the area, that facility used to be a home care service business. However, as the prison became overcrowded, they converted that building as well.

The multiple buildings on the grounds didn't worry Razor, though. They had more than enough people to overpower the prison guards. Like before, Cole gave the growing group a speech about changing history and correcting the wrongs of this country, letting the government hear our anger and frustration, and showing them that all of its citizens are standing united. The crowd was fired up; they stormed the prison grounds and overwhelmed the guards there.

The prisoners were quickly released. Again, they eagerly wanted to join the fight. Everything was going smoothly. A part of him still waited for the other shoe to drop, but this time Razor didn't think it would. Either way, he was ready for it.

Now, they were in Lansing, specifically at Hawk Island Park. No, the location wasn't ideal for Helena, but it was the only place big enough to hold their ever-growing group. The plan was still to conduct raids, but it also involved Cole going around to rally the public. Public speeches were never considered a crime. It was just that no one was around who cared to listen. No one wanted to draw attention to themselves, especially if it meant going against the system. However, in this case, that's precisely what they aimed to do.

"Overwhelm the residents all at once," Razor told the small group. Cole, Jackson, Zara, Brice, Keeper, Tatianna, Helena, Sunday, Yoko, Clay, Reagan, and Jade all sat with him around the campfire. "While Cole gives his speech at Debbie Stabenow Park, one team will be raiding a sweep happening in the Old Everett neighborhood, another team will conduct a raid in the Georgetown Park area, and the last team will be in Moores Park," he explained.

"That sounds overwhelming," Tatianna said.

"I'll lead the team at Moores Park," Jade said.

"I'll take Old Everett," Jackson volunteered.

"I suppose that'll leave Georgetown Park to me," Keeper said.

"Sounds good," Razor said, pleased.

"What's the endgame here?" Jade asked. It seemed like this was the first time she was talking to him directly. "Is there a reason for the overwhelming tactics?"

"The plan is to dismantle Lansing's stronghold, the Greater Lansing Prison."

"That is something," Cole sighed.

"That place is enormous," Tatianna said.

"Does any part of it still serve as a hospital?" Keeper asked.

"It's rumored that only the top floor still functions as a hospital," Razor said. "But who knows if that's really true?"

"If we want it to go smoothly, we're going to need more people," Helena said.

"But this is the capital," Jade said. "Who's to say the government officials won't send the military after us?"

"That's why we're having Cole deliver his speeches," Razor said. "If the officials see how much support he's getting from the citizens, they'll hesitate before launching an attack on us."

"That doesn't sound like they won't do it, though," Jade countered.

"No, but we'll be ready for it regardless."

"Besides," Tatianna said. "With the people we'll gain from these sweeps, and the folks from the prison, I bet we'll be able to overwhelm them."

"Yeah," Keeper chimed in. "After breaking out the prisoners from the Greater Lansing Prison, there'll be no stopping us."

"Alright," Razor said, looking at everyone. "Gather your groups, let them know the plan, and we'll head out at daybreak."

Jade was the first to get up and walk away. The others gradually followed. Helena sighed as her sister moved further out of her line of sight. Razor stayed silent. Only Sunday and Cole remained with them.

"And the tantrum continues," Sunday grumbled.

"How are you feeling, Helena?" Cole asked.

"I'm actually feeling good today," Helena smiled. Razor was relieved to hear that. He tried to hide it, but Helena's pregnancy symptoms frightened him. Cole assured him that everything was normal, but that never eased his worries. So hearing Helena say she was having a good day gave him a little hope.

"Wonderful," Cole said. "I want you and Sunday to come with me tomorrow."

"We would love to," Helena said.

"You have a way with words," Sunday added.

Cole laughed. "Thank you, Sunday," he looked over at Razor. "And where will you be?"

"I haven't decided yet."

"Ah, I see," Cole nodded. "Well, either way, Helena will be in good hands. I'll see you all at daybreak," Cole said before walking away.

"You'll be with Helena, of course," Sunday glared.

"Or with Jade," Razor said. Even though he believed that Jade's distance would be for the best, Razor was still irritated by the whole situation. He hated it when she pulled away from him. She could be angry with him all she wanted, but staying away was unacceptable. He needed to find a way to bring her back.

"Don't give in to that big baby," Sunday snapped. "Focus on your family."

"Jade is my family," Razor sighed. Sunday seemed to be angrier with Jade than Helena was.

"Well, she's not acting like it," she said, rubbing Helena's back for comfort.

"I'll get her to come around," Razor said. "I've done it before."

Sunday rolled her eyes but didn't say anything. Razor smiled. Although she drove him crazy to no end, Razor appreciated Sunday. He could even say that he loved her. Even when there were moments he couldn't understand her, he was still glad she was there.

"Whether I'm there or not, focus on supporting Helena, ok?" Razor said as he knelt before her.

"Of course," Sunday said with a smile. Razor patted the top of her head, and she frowned. She quickly swatted his hand away. "Stop that!"

Razor laughed, then kissed the top of her head. "Thank you."

"You two are so cute," Helena said.

Razor stood up, wrapped Helena in his arms, and kissed her passionately. Helena responded by grabbing his hair and pulling him even closer. Razor held back a laugh. He loved it when she became aggressive with him.

"Ew, get a room," Sunday said as she walked away.

Helena shyly pulled back from their kiss. It left Razor craving even more.

"It'd be nice if you weren't in ours all the time!" Razor teased as Sunday was a little further away from them. She responded with a middle finger. Razor laughed.

"I think that might've bought us a little alone time," Helena said, giving Razor a certain look.

"Lead the way," Razor smiled. He would fix things with Jade soon enough, but for now, Razor would enjoy this moment with his wife.

~24~

Helena

The camp was lively despite it still being dark outside. It was early morning, and everyone was preparing to depart for their respective destinations at daybreak. Sunday was helping Helena into the fighting corset Keeper had made for her. She started to notice how much her stomach was beginning to protrude. It wasn't very noticeable, but it was enough for Helena to feel it, making it all the more real.

Helena felt exhausted. She hardly got any sleep during the night, and it wasn't because of her pregnancy. It was Jade's distance. Ever since the first raid in Dimondale, Jade had been keeping her distance from her. Jade would only ask Helena how she was feeling, and then she'd march off once she got an answer. Helena understood that Jade was angry with Razor, but she didn't realize that the feeling would extend to her as well. She hadn't done anything wrong in the situation. So, why was she getting the cold shoulder right now? Helena was determined to find out.

Once Sunday was done helping Helena put on her fighting corset, Helena finished dressing, gathered her weapons, and headed to Jade's tent. Razor was already up and out, meeting with Cole and Bossman at Cavanaugh Park. Bossman was hiding out there, which was a mile and a half from where they stayed. He was close, but not too close to the debtors. That was something. But Helena knew it wasn't enough for Jade.

"Sunday, I need a huge favor from you," Helena said as they walked toward Jade's tent.

"Anything," Sunday said ecstatically.

"Don't say anything during this conversation," Helena sighed. "I don't want Jade to feel like we're ganging up on her."

Sunday bit her lip and nodded. "Ok."

"Promise?" Helena asked. She really needed Sunday to stay quiet. She was a little firecracker, and their argument was bound to set her off.

"I promise, Helena," Sunday said. "I won't add any more stress on you."

"Thank you, Sunday."

They reached Jade's tent, and Helena paused quietly at the entrance for a moment. She felt nervous; her stomach twisted in knots. Luckily, the tent's entrance was zipped shut, so Jade didn't have to see Helena standing there frozen. Helena took a few deep breaths and mustered her courage.

"Knock, knock," Helena said with a shaky voice. Sunday responded by rubbing Helena's back. She didn't know how Sunday knew, but Helena found the action very comforting.

No one responded, but the tent flaps were being unzipped, and Clay was stepping out. He smiled shyly at them.

"Morning," he greeted them.

"Hey," Helena sighed. "I wanted to talk to my sister."

"She's in there getting dressed," he said as he moved aside to let Helena through. "I'm going to meet up with Reagan." He quickly walked off.

Helena took another deep breath before stepping inside. Sunday silently followed. Jade's back was to her as she was placing knives into her thigh straps and knife holster belt, which Keeper made.

"Hey, can we talk?" Helena asked.

"How are you feeling?" Jade asked without looking at her.

"Not great," Helena sighed.

"You should see Cole or Keeper."

"It has nothing to do with the pregnancy. This is about how you've been treating me."

"Let's not, Helena."

"No, let's, Jade!" Helena snapped. Jade's tone was so condescending that Helena didn't know whether she should be angry or hurt. "What have I possibly done to make you treat me this way?!"

"I'm tired of hearing the same old bullshit from all of you!" Jade turned around, face enraged. "Calm down, Jade! Don't be so angry, Jade! Look at the bigger picture, Jade! Fuck all of that!"

"This means more than just you."

"I don't fucking care!" Jade snapped. "All I want is my revenge! I'm not so quick to forgive that psycho like the rest of you!"

"No one has forgiven him," Helena cried. "Jesus, Jade, how could you say that?! You're not the only person here who's hurting. I miss Raina, Levi, and David, too. But other things are happening in my life, and I'm scared. And right now, I need my big sister by my side."

"They don't visit me anymore," Jade cried. "They used to visit me, talk to me, comfort me. And they stopped. They left me for good."

"They're always with you, Jade."

"They were my family," Jade continued as if Helena hadn't spoken. "And now they're gone."

Helena frowned as she listened to Jade's words. "What about me? Am I no longer your family? Is me being alive not enough for you?"

Jade sighed and rolled her eyes. "That's not what I meant, Helena."

"Then what did you mean?!" Helena snapped, tears running down her face.

"It's never going to be enough," Jade said after a long pause. "Without them here, I'll never feel complete."

Helena felt her heart break as she looked at her sister. She wasn't enough for her. That was the most hurtful thing she's ever heard. Whether she intended to or not, Jade crushed her.

"Thank you for that, Jade," Helena said, wiping her tears and slowly backing away. "Thank you for abandoning me once again."

Helena spun around in a blind rage. Luckily, Sunday grabbed her hand and pulled her out of the tent. Helena could hear Jade calling after her, but Sunday was walking quickly.

"Your girlfriend's a dick!" Sunday shouted to Clay as they hurried past him.

Helena could only focus on her breathing. It was taking all her strength not to break down and have a panic attack. She could hear voices and movement around her, but she couldn't focus on it all. Suddenly, Sunday stood guard in front of Helena, her knife pointed at Jade.

"Don't you dare come near her!" Sunday shouted. "You made your choice! Now stay the fuck away from Helena!"

Clay was pulling Jade away while Tatianna stood in front of Sunday. Helena diverted her gaze to the ground because she didn't want to look at Jade; she didn't have the strength to do so.

"Hey, is everything ok?" Tatianna asked as she placed a hand on her shoulder.

"No, Tati," Helena broke down. "Nothing is ok."

~25~

Clay

As the group started their three-mile trip to Debbie Stabenow Park, Clay couldn't take his eyes off Helena. She was doing her best, trying to hold her head high and pretend nothing had happened. At first, Clay had planned to go with Jade and raid the sweep in the Moores Park area, but after this morning's incident, he thought it would be better to go with Helena. While Helena didn't seem to mind him being there, Sunday, on the other hand, looked annoyed. It was funny; when he first met her, she seemed protective of Jade, but that changed quickly.

"No more! No more! This President has got to go!" the crowd chanted as they marched to the park. "No more! No more! This President has got to go!"

Clay watched as Helena chanted the statement with the crowd. Even though he saw her lips moving, he could barely hear her voice. It was obvious she was just going through the motions.

"Keep your eyes on where you're going," Sunday said, glaring at him.

Clay nodded and looked ahead.

"No more! No more! This President has got to go!"

"Why aren't you with your dick-of-a-girlfriend?" she grumbled.

Clay chuckled. "Needed a change of scenery."

"Yeah, well, don't bother Helena," Sunday demanded. "She's already upset enough."

"No more! No more! This President has got to go!"

Sunday joined the chant, and Clay followed. As they passed abandoned buildings and houses, people slowly started to emerge. It was unusual to see a group marching and protesting. The group was out and making themselves noticed. That was not something you did anymore, even in the Capital. Yes, the capital city was very different from other cities, but there were still debtors. Even ordinary citizens preferred to stay out of sight.

"No more! No more! This President has got to go!"

Some people started to approach the crowd. Some group members greeted them and encouraged them to join in and listen to Cole's speech at the park. Almost everyone who approached the crowd eventually joined the group and walked to the park. Clay was impressed. Cole had a strong influence over the people, and that influence eventually spread to those who followed him.

"No more! No more! This President has got to go!"

By the time they reached the park, the crowd had grown quite large. Word must have spread, because when they arrived at the spot where Cole was supposed to give his speech, people were already gathered and waiting. A few Black Coats members helped Cole onto a boulder where he planned to deliver his speech.

"No more! No more! This President has got to go!"

"I know you came to comfort me," Helena said as she took Clay's hand in hers. Her eyes were forward, watching Cole. "But, I've come to terms with it."

"No more! No more! This President has got to go!"

Clay looked at her. She was trying to hide it, but he noticed how glossy her eyes were. "Come to terms with what?"

"No more! No more! This President has got to go!"

"That I have to do all of this without her," Helena's free hand moved to her belly. Sunday, who was on the other side of Helena, started rubbing her back. "I didn't see it before, but now I realize I lost a big part of Jade on the Detroit River that night."

"No more! No more! This President has got to go!"

Clay only responded by squeezing Helena's hand. Helena looked at him and smiled. With her smile and the way her watery, brown eyes shimmered in that moment, Clay completely understood why Razor fell in love with her. What was it about the Willer sisters that made them so captivating?

"No more! No more! This President has got to go!"

"Can you promise me something, Clay?" she asked.

"Anything."

"No more! No more! This President has got to go!"

"Keep being there for Jade."

Clay nodded. "I will."

"No more! No more! This President has got to go!"

Helena sighed and rested her head on his arm. Clay kissed the top of her head and stayed there, taking in the sweet scent of her hair. It was calming. He risked getting a beating from Razor, but the peaceful smile on Helena's face made the risk worth it. As long as he was comforting Helena, Clay considered it a job well done.

"No more! No more! This President has got to go!"

Cole raised his hand to quiet the crowd. "It brings me great joy to see all of you here today," Cole said, smiling. "Just by being here, you're showing how fed up you are with this system and its disgusting laws!"

The crowd cheered.

"The amount of courage you've shown by walking out of your hideouts, marching beside us, and listening to what I have to say, gives me so much hope." Cole paused to look at the crowd. It seemed like he wanted to take the time to look at everyone directly. Clay noticed that some people burst into tears when Cole's eyes fell upon them. "The time has come to fight back! The time has come to show this country that we want our freedom back! The time has come to rebuild our democracy!"

The crowd shouted and applauded.

"It's time to tell this government that we, the people, are taking this country back from them! They have misused and abused this system enough! We are tired of being on the brutal end of their corruption! We are tired of suffering the consequences for their own personal gains!"

"We've had enough!"

"No more!"

"No more!"

"This President has got to go!"

"It is time to remind this regime that they work for us! Let us remind them that they are here to serve us! They are meant to protect us! And if they do not comply, we will burn this place to the ground!"

More cheers erupted.

"Show them that we are not afraid to dismantle this system and rebuild! Let them know that we have no fear of dragging them out of their offices and replacing them with those who are unafraid! With those who will not bend the knee! With those who will protect and serve the people! We, the people, have built this country! We, the people, have loved this country! And we, the people, refuse to be terrorized by it again!"

"We refuse!" someone shouted.

"We refuse! We refuse! We refuse!" the crowd started chanting.

Helena lifted her head from Clay's arm and glanced around. "Wow."

"We refuse! We refuse! We refuse!"

"I know," Clay said. The atmosphere was electric.

"We refuse! We refuse! We refuse!"

"This country is in desperate need of new leadership," Cole said once the crowd quieted down. "And I, Dr. Cole Blackwell, would like to take on that role. I want to erase the stain of red this country has left, and lead you all into an era of black."

"Into the black!" a Black Coats member shouted.

"Into the black! Into the black! Into the black!"

Clay observed a few people pushing through the crowd, trying to reach the front. They were wearing suits, which Clay found a bit strange. A member of the Black Coats immediately stopped them before they got too close to Cole. Cole looked down at them, smiling, and said something. Of course, Clay couldn't hear over the chanting crowd.

"Into the black! Into the black! Into the black!"

"Oh my God," Helena gasped.

Clay quickly turned to her. "What's wrong?"

"Is the baby ok?" Sunday asked, panicking.

"Into the black! Into the black! Into the black!"

"Those are senators," Helena said. "I forget their names, but I know they're really important."

"Into the black! Into the black! Into the black!"

"Well," Clay said, looking back at them. Cole was now off the boulder and still talking to them. It appeared to be a friendly conversation. And then, they all shook hands. "This just got even more interesting."

"Into the black! Into the black! Into the black!"

~26~

Razor

The area around Moores Park was intriguing. The most fascinating thing was the operational dam. Razor watched as the water flowed through it. It was strangely captivating. Or maybe it was just distracting him from trying to figure out what happened between Helena and Jade. Razor knew it was serious. Sunday refused to repeat what was said, and Clay only insisted on going with Helena. That's how Razor knew it was bad. If Clay was choosing Helena over Jade, a line had to have been crossed. And Razor didn't know what to do with that realization.

"Can you at least look at me?" Jade asked. He knew she'd been watching him but avoided looking back at her. She had been trying to talk to him the whole way there. But Razor knew his anger, and he didn't want to hear anything that might upset him.

"Just fix it," he said, finally looking over at her. Her eyes were red, so he knew she'd been crying. Yup, it was bad.

"I don't know if I can," she said, looking guilty.

The best part of the park's location was that it was right in the middle of a neighborhood. So their group was spread out, stationed at every corner. It was easy to intervene and protect the debtors. Their position was perfect, which is why Razor was completely fine with him and Jade being in this area alone.

"Then I support whatever decision Helena makes," Razor said.

Jade's expression of guilt shifted into anger. "Fine," she snapped.

"Do you know what your problem is, Jade?"

"Oh, please tell me, Razor! What more do I need to work on?"

"You stay stuck in the past," he said calmly. "We're trying to focus on creating a better future, and you're pissed at us for it. You know the stakes we're facing if we don't pull this off, and yet you still don't care. It's all about satisfying your need for revenge, and it hurts."

"Yeah, well, you're the only one getting a happy ending out of this."

"The growth of your family isn't a happy ending for you?" Razor raised an eyebrow.

Jade rolled her eyes. "That's not what I meant."

"Then what is it, Jade? Because I'm getting fucking tired of this."

Jade didn't answer. Razor couldn't tell if she was refusing or if she simply didn't have one.

He sighed. "I love you, Jade—more than you could possibly know. But if you make me choose between you and Helena, I'm choosing Helena every single time."

"Yeah, I got that," she said, storming off.

Razor tried to hide his disappointment. This wasn't how he wanted to handle things, but Jade was leaving him no other option. In truth, he would try to find a way to keep both of them. He couldn't imagine a life without Jade. He loved her too much to let her go. Still, he hoped his statement about choosing Helena would be the push Jade needed to get herself together.

But deep down, he knew it wouldn't work. Not with someone as stubborn as Jade.

After a few minutes, Razor went after her. She hadn't gone far, just pacing near the tree line that separates the park from the neighborhood. Jade saw him approaching and stopped pacing.

"I'm done talking, Razor," she cried.

Razor grabbed her by the arm and pulled her close. "You don't have the right to just distance yourself from us," he snapped. He could feel her heavy breaths on his chest as he looked down at her. She avoided meeting his gaze. He had to get through to her. Razor needed Jade to realize that keeping her distance from them frustrated him.

"You'll choose Helena, remember?" Her voice cracked as she struggled to free herself from his hold. Razor tightened his grip.

"Fuck, Jade, do you really believe that?" Razor's voice now cracked. He was doing everything he could to keep his emotions in check, but he was failing. "I'd probably die trying to pick you both!"

Jade stopped resisting. "It's just..." She struggled to catch her breath. "I'm just so angry all the time, Razor. I don't feel at peace. I know what you're trying to do is important, and it needs to be done. But I can't get past my anger to care."

Razor wrapped her in his arms as she broke down crying. He buried his face in her hair as tears fell from his eyes. It was amazing how she and Helena both had a similar scent. That small detail comforted him whenever he embraced them. It was tough knowing there were no words he could offer Jade to soothe her. Until she could take revenge on Nick, she wouldn't find relief. All Razor could do was offer a shoulder to cry on.

"I love you so much, Jade," he said after a moment. "So, please, don't make me choose."

Jade held onto him tightly and looked up at him with teary eyes. "That's the problem, Razor. You love me so much that it might be the death of you."

The statement should have scared Razor, but he was too focused on how beautiful she looked in that moment.

**

The raid was successful. There were more than enough people to overpower the small number of officers conducting the sweep. After they stopped the sweep from happening, Jade and the others convinced the group of debtors to join them in the fight. Some people declined and went back into hiding. Others agreed to join and followed Jade as she led them back to Hawk Island Park.

Razor felt less stressed as he made his way back. He'd finally gotten through to Jade. He wasn't sure if things between her and Helena would be the same, but at least Jade wouldn't be avoiding them. Now, he just needed to check in with Helena. But as he reached the park's entrance, Razor realized that the task would have to wait. Cole and Clay were standing there, and it looked like they were waiting for him.

"We need to have an important chat, my friend," Cole greeted him.

Razor observed that Clay only nodded in greeting to Jade.

"My tent or yours?" Razor asked.

"This needs to be discussed off-site," Cole said as he walked out of the park.

Razor sighed as he followed. He was really hoping to talk to Helena first. "How's she doing?" Razor asked Clay as they walked side by side.

"Better," Clay said.

"Do I want to know what was said between them?"

"Not really."

Razor sighed again. He had come to realize that Clay wasn't much of a talker. The most he ever talked to him was the time Clay admitted he had feelings for Jade. Razor wondered what he and Jade had actually discussed. Then Razor noticed the direction they were heading. He had initially thought their conversation would be with Nick at Cavanaugh Park. But instead of heading west, they were going south.

"Where are we headed?" Razor asked.

"I couldn't bring them to our base," Cole said over his shoulder. "And I definitely couldn't take them to the other park. So, I settled on this place instead."

The men walked quietly for a moment until they saw a playground with a roofed picnic area. Three people were gathered there. Two sat at a table, while the third paced back and forth. All of them looked at the men as they approached. As they got closer, Razor realized they were three senators: Senator Gina Shields, Senator Joel Weins, and Senator Morris Bunte. They were all well known for opposing President Chase Dooms and the DC task force.

"I must say," Razor said as he approached them. "I'm surprised to see you all here, senators."

"I never thought I'd see the day when the legendary Razor Thompson became a wanted man because he was fighting against the system he helped create," Senator Gina Shields said as she stopped pacing.

"If I'm not mistaken, Senator Shields, the vote to approve the DC task force was unanimous," Razor shot back.

"None of us knew that it would escalate to this point," Senator Morris Bunte said as he stood from the table.

"We all thought we would just be preserving our medical care resources," Senator Joel Weins sighed, still sitting.

"But these horrors have lasted long enough, don't you think?" Gina said as she gestured for Razor to sit.

Razor sat across from the others at the table, along with Cole and Clay.

"Thank you for bringing him, Dr. Blackwell," Gina said as she sat down.

"Of course, Senator Shields," Cole said, smiling and folding his hands on the table. "But I have to admit it was for selfish reasons. I'm more interested in what you have to say."

"The news of what you all are doing is spreading like wildfire," Gina started.

"It's giving many people hope and courage," Morris added. "They are protesting and fighting back in the streets."

"They're even starting to take a page out of your playbook by raiding the sweeps," Joel said. "And with the limited number of DC officers now, they've all been successful."

"So, what do you want from us?" Razor asked. He could sense a request coming.

"You need to deliver a final blow," Gina said. "Something monumental."

"The raids and the prison breaks aren't enough?" Cole asked.

"While they were prison breaks," Joel said. "They weren't big enough, and they definitely weren't secure enough."

"It has to be a bigger message," Morris stated.

"To whom exactly?" Clay asked. Razor noticed a bit of annoyance in his tone. "You said the people are fighting back. That's who we're delivering our message to."

"You also want to send one to the rest of the senators," Gina said.

"And what are we supposed to expect from them?" It was clear that Clay didn't like the senators, and Razor couldn't blame him.

"It will make them turn against President Dooms," Gina smiled.

"Bullshit," Clay scoffed.

Senator Shields stood up and started pacing again. "I understand why you'd be worried about them turning," she said after a few seconds.

"Can you blame me?" Clay glared. "They haven't done shit since the DCs started terrorizing."

"A lot of them felt like there was nothing they could do," Morris explained. "Anyone who spoke against President Dooms and the DC task force was eventually interrogated."

"Surely, you know this, Razor," Joel said, looking at him for validation.

"Although I've never seen it myself, rumors have circulated," Razor sighed. Of course, he knew the truth. Razor was sure Nick had carried out a few "interrogations" himself. However, Razor didn't know just how many were done on these senators.

"I have to wonder," Cole said, taking his time to look at the senators. "Why were the three of you spared from these interrogations?"

"Good question," Razor mumbled.

"Because the number of people who support us," Gina said. "Here in Michigan, we've had many government officials who supported our views."

"The senators who were interrogated were outliers in their states," Joel explained. "So it was easy for it to go ignored if they temporarily went missing."

"And no one questioned when they began singing a different tune,"

Morris added.

"Or stopped saying anything altogether," Gina also added.

"But it'd be too big to ignore if you three started doing that," Cole stated.

"Exactly," Gina said. "That's why you need to do something big, Dr. Blackwell. If you weaken President Dooms' major policy, then the other senators will have no problem backing you as the new president."

"Why wouldn't one of the other senators try to get elected?" Clay asked, still unconvinced.

At this, all the senators laughed. Gina looked over at Clay and gave him a sympathetic look.

"No one wants to lead during this troubling time," she chuckled.

"It's too much work," Joel admitted.

"It's how we ended up with President Dooms in the first place," Morris sighed. "No one wanted the headache of trying to figure everything out."

Clay scoffed and shook his head.

"We have a plan," Razor said. "We just need more time and more people before we can execute it."

Gina nodded. "That's great to hear because word has it, President Dooms will be making his way here."

"And how we hear it, he's planning to do a hostile takeover of the Capitol building," Morris said, looking around as if he expected someone to overhear.

"So we really need people to rally together to prevent that from happening," Joel said.

"You're really asking a lot from the people, aren't you?" Clay said sharply.

"Unfortunately, nothing will change unless the people fight back," Gina sighed. "It has to be you."

"Yeah," Clay said, getting up. "Maybe we should look into getting rid of all of you, too."

"I must say, fresh blood does sound nice," Cole said, following Clay's lead.

Razor stood up as well. "I think that concludes this meeting," he said, watching the senators prepare to leave. "Keep your ears to the ground and gather up people around the Capitol building. Once we make our move, we will head there."

"Thank you, Razor," Gina smiled.

"Just be sure to make Cole president once all of this is done," Razor said before walking off. His mind was racing. Chase was planning a hostile takeover of the Capitol building. They needed to move quickly.

~27~

Jade

Over the next few days, Jade desperately tried to make amends with Helena. It wasn't that Helena was ignoring her completely, but her interactions with her sister felt different. When Sunday wasn't intervening, Helena's interactions appeared nonchalant and distant. She wasn't acting like herself. While Jade was glad she wasn't being ignored, she wished things between them could go back to how they used to be.

Of course, there was no one to blame but herself. Jade should've never said she wasn't complete without David, Raina, and Levi. What was she thinking? Yes, she felt their loss deeply, but losing Helena or Razor would've broken her completely. She hated that she made Helena feel otherwise. Jade was so angry about the Bossman situation that she wanted those around her to be hurt. But she went too far with Helena. Those words should've never crossed her mind, much less been spoken. Now Jade was paying for them.

Jade walked over to Helena and Razor's tent. She was meeting Razor to head to Cavanaugh Park, where Bossman was living. Razor, Cole, and Bossman planned to review their strategy for the prison break at Greater Lansing Prison. Since they would likely be split into different teams, Razor wanted Jade to be there as an extra set of ears so she could accurately relay the plan.

As Jade approached Helena's tent, Sunday was walking out of her small, makeshift one nearby. Sunday looked at Jade with indifference. Jade knew she had let her down. Sunday had once admired her; now, Jade was a huge disappointment. Jade couldn't really blame her for feeling that way.

"Razor isn't in there," Sunday said, crossing her arms.

"I wanted to check on Helena."

"The doc said she's doing well. And she woke up in good spirits today, so leave her be."

"Sunday..." Jade pleaded.

"No," Sunday snapped. "You don't get to hurt her and pretend like everything's good."

"I'm not pretending. I want to make it right. I never meant to hurt—"

"Oh, eat shit!" Sunday yelled, cutting her off. "You definitely meant to hurt her! All you care about is revenge. So go get it and leave us alone!"

Jade watched as Sunday stormed into Helena's tent. For a brief moment, Jade saw Helena sitting on a cot with her arms open, inviting Sunday in. Jade felt her heart break. How could she let Helena down again? It seemed like she had come full circle. She had spent so much time amid this chaos trying to find and support her sister, vowing never to let her down again, and now she does this?

What the hell was wrong with her?

Had her need for blood really driven her to do this? Jade sighed as she walked away. She had a sinking feeling with every step she took. This time, she felt like she wouldn't have the chance to make it up to Helena. And that thought scared her.

**

"Any ETA on when Chase will get to the State Capitol?" Razor asked Bossman.

Jade, Razor, Cole, Zara, and Bossman were all sitting around a small campfire. Bossman was in the middle of preparing lunch when they arrived.

"Unfortunately, I've gotten radio silence," Bossman said, finishing his piece of fish.

"Does he have enough people to take over the Capitol?" Jade asked. "I mean, we've been seeing the number of DC officers dwindle."

"The same can't be said for the military," Razor sighed.

"Well," Bossman licked his fingers and set his plate down. "I can attest that he doesn't have the full backing and support of the soldiers."

"And how do you know this?" Jade frowned. Everything about him was making her angry and disgusted.

"I've had interactions with them," he shrugged. "Anyway, I've heard that he may be using the remaining Radical members who are still around."

"Why would they even bother?" Zara asked. "This has nothing to do with them."

"Simple, revenge," Bossman said. "We did take out a large number of their group, including their leaders."

"Not to mention, many of their members are also American," Cole sighed.

Great. Jade was beginning to think they wouldn't ever get rid of the Radicals.

"This will affect our plans," Razor frowned. Jade could tell he was deep in thought.

"Here's what I propose," Bossman said. "We attack the prison and the State Capitol at the same time."

"But we don't know if Chase will show up," Razor said.

"We'll make sure he's there," Bossman smirked.

"How?" Jade hated it when he took his time explaining his plans.

"The doc does what he does best, he gives a speech at the Capitol," Bossman leaned back with satisfaction. "We announce that he will give a speech on a specific date and time. We have a group hidden in the crowd. While Chase is there taking the bait, the other group will be carrying out the prison break, making Chase look even weaker."

Razor nodded as he considered this. Jade believed the plan was solid, but she wondered where Bossman would be during all of this.

"I don't see you sitting this one out," Jade said, glaring at him.

"Oh, I won't be, my sweet Jade," he chuckled. "I will be at the Capitol, ready to kill Chase."

Jade sighed and rolled her eyes.

"He's tried to kill me," Bossman suddenly snapped. "I do not intend for that to go unanswered!"

"Besides," Zara sighed. "We can't expect Cole to kill him. That wouldn't look good."

"I don't care whether or not President Dooms dies," Jade said. "I don't think Bossman should be around the debtors."

"I won't be."

"Good," Jade crossed her arms. "And I'll be there to make sure of it."

"I'm all for a plan that gives me time with you, my love," Bossman smiled, his mood shifted.

Jade didn't snap at him for calling her his love; she didn't care to. She had found her moment—the perfect chance to kill him. Once he killed President Dooms, Jade would take out Bossman. She would finally get her revenge, and that would be the end of it.

**

After dinner, Jade returned to her tent to lie down and pout. Razor had gone over the plan with everyone, splitting them into groups and assigning locations. Naturally, she and Helena were in different groups and at separate locations. Not that she could really blame Razor for it. Jade was determined to keep an eye on Bossman at the Capitol, while Razor was more worried about the prison break. So, of course, they wouldn't be together. Still, it seemed like Jade was prioritizing her revenge over Helena. This didn't look good for her case.

Jade was running out of time to repair her relationship with her sister. She needed to act quickly. There were only three days before they carried out their plan. Group members were going out and making announcements about Cole's speech at the State Capitol. They aimed to attract attention. And once they did, everything would escalate fast. Jade needed to make the most of this brief window.

"Still haven't come up with a solution, I see," Clay said, lying beside her. He started planting kisses on Jade's neck.

Jade smiled. She enjoyed the warmth and softness of his lips against her skin. She appreciated many things about him, such as the way he said her name when they kissed, the feel of his rough hands sliding over her skin during their embrace, and how his brown eyes seemed to sparkle as he looked down at her.

Clay positioned himself between her legs as Jade wrapped her arms around his neck. Their kisses were always passionate, as if they were kissing each other for the last time. This time was no exception. Jade's hold on his neck grew tighter as she deepened their kiss. She needed to feel closer to him. She needed to feel secure. Whenever they were intimate, Jade constantly yearned for more. There were times when she wanted to be so close to him that she didn't know where he ended and she began. When it came to him, she could never get enough.

Clay was the first to pull away. Jade could immediately sense the loneliness in the space he created. She took deep breaths as she tried to clear her mind. She needed to focus on her dilemma with Helena. Clay chuckled as he watched her struggle. He resumed kissing her neck.

"What's tripping you up?" he asked between kisses.

"H-how to get her t-to forgive me," she stammered. Jade could hear his low, rough chuckle in her ear. It was a while before he spoke again, because his tongue was making slow circles along Jade's neck, which sent shivers down her spine.

"Maybe you're focusing on the wrong thing," he said before slipping his tongue into her mouth. Jade dug her nails into his back and let out a soft moan in response. Clay pulled away, and Jade groaned in protest. He smiled at her. "Instead of trying to get Helena's forgiveness, try telling her how you feel," he said. "And let her decide what she wants to do from there."

"But what if she decides she wants nothing to do with me?" Jade's heart raced at that thought.

Clay slowly sat up. The distance between them became palpable. He shrugged. "Then it's something you'd have to live with."

Jade feared that response. She knew it could be a possible outcome, but hearing it aloud terrified her. She also knew Clay was disappointed in how she treated Helena, but his reaction made her realize just how disappointed he truly was.

"Ok," she said. "I have to be ready to live with it."

**

The odds seemed to favor her as Helena arrived at Jade's tent that evening. Clay was headed out to speak with Reagan when she stopped by. Helena's face brightened upon seeing him. Clay embraced her warmly and kissed her forehead quickly. He told Helena he was going to see Reagan and then headed off. Helena watched him go.

Jade knew they had become close when she and Razor were away, and it seemed like Clay was still taking care of her. That was reassuring to know. Helena deserved all the support.

It wasn't until Clay was out of view that Helena looked at Jade.

"I've come to do your hair," Helena said. All the warmth Helena once showed toward Clay was now gone.

"Sure," Jade smiled weakly. "As you wish." Jade quickly sat on one of the stools in the tent. Usually, she would've groaned about it, but that wasn't an option for her. She needed Helena in a good mood.

Helena stood behind her and began undoing one of her braids. They both remained silent for a moment. Jade didn't know how to start. She felt so nervous right then.

"Are you good with standing?" Jade asked after a while. Helena had already rebraided two braids.

"I won't be long."

"Ok," Jade began, nervously picking at one of her fingernails. "Look, Helena—"

"You're sorry, you didn't mean it like *that*," Helena interrupted. "I got it, Jade."

"Just let me explain," Jade pleaded. Helena didn't say anything. She started unraveling the third braid. Jade saw this as a sign to keep going. "You and Razor mean everything to me. I was so consumed by my anger that I started seeing everyone who opposed me as the enemy. And I said those things only to hurt you."

Jade paused to see if Helena would react to what she said. Helena just focused on her braiding.

"That was really shitty of me and totally unfair to you. I'm just scared, Helena. I'm so afraid of losing you and Razor, and I'm terrified of losing your baby," Jade sighed. "And if Bossman is still alive when it comes, then I feel like I've failed at protecting my family. He can't be here when they're born, Helena. The world isn't safe for them if he's around."

Several minutes passed before Helena acknowledged Jade's statement. Jade had started to think she would never get a response and was too wary to push the issue. Finally, Helena spoke as she worked on the last braid.

"Do what you have to do, Jade. But I've made peace and am content with the part of you you've chosen to give."

Jade frowned at the statement. What did Helena mean by that? Had she not given Helena all of herself? Jade thought she had, but apparently she was wrong. All of this felt so wrong.

When Helena finished fixing her hair, she wrapped her arms around Jade and kissed her on the cheek. "I love you, Jade. Nothing you do could change that."

Tears streamed from Jade's eyes. This didn't feel like forgiveness; it felt like accepting the new, strange relationship Jade had pushed them into. Because her spiteful words catapulted them into it, Jade had no choice but to accept it as well.

"I love you, too, Helena," Jade sighed. "And I'm so sorry that I'm not always good to you."

~28~

Jade

During the time Jade had known Reagan, she could never remember a moment when she saw her angry, not even when she was fighting DC officers and Radical members. But Reagan was furious now, and it scared Jade a little. Jade and Clay were about to leave to travel to the State Capitol with Bossman. Reagan was upset about her brother being alone with him. Jade tried to convince Clay to travel with Cole's group. Just because she was determined to keep an eye on Bossman didn't mean Clay had to be subjected to him, too. But Clay wasn't interested in the idea. If Jade was traveling with Bossman, then so was he.

"Are you trying to get yourself killed?" Reagan asked her brother as she glared at him. They stood outside their tent. Jade and Clay had packed up for their trip.

"And you're ok with Jade being in danger?" Clay shot back.

Reagan rolled her eyes. "Oh, please. If Bossman wanted to kill Jade, she'd be dead already."

Clay remained silent, and Jade did the same.

"Aside from Razor, Jade is the only one safe to be around him," Reagan continued.

"Reagan, this is happening, despite what you say," Clay said in a tone that conveyed the end of the conversation.

Reagan sighed and then nodded. She went over and hugged her brother. Jade could see how worried and anxious Reagan was. It made Jade feel bad. She felt like she was taking Clay away from Reagan.

"Stay alert out there," Reagan said after they finished hugging.

"You too," Clay smiled. "And stay close to Helena. Make sure she doesn't go too far."

Reagan nodded in understanding. Jade frowned as she tried to figure out what he meant. Reagan went over to hug her.

"Take care of him," Reagan whispered in her ear.

"I will," Jade said, releasing Reagan from her embrace just as Helena, Sunday, and Razor approached them.

Helena immediately hugged Jade tightly, and Jade responded in kind. She hated that she wouldn't be fighting alongside Helena—and hated even more that she was the one who made that decision.

"Stay safe," Jade whispered. "And don't rush in if you don't have to."

Helena nodded. Once they let go of each other, Helena quickly wiped away the tears that had fallen. Sunday gave Jade a quick hug.

"Do what you have to do," Sunday said.

Jade nodded.

It was Razor's turn to embrace Jade. "Stay sharp. Hold Chase back until we get there."

"I will."

"I love you," Razor said, kissing her forehead.

"I love you, too," Jade said, looking at everyone. "I love all of you."

Helena's eyes teared up as she looked at Jade. "I love you more, Jade."

**

Jade walked with a heavy heart. She didn't think her goodbyes would be so painful. She couldn't understand why. Maybe it was because she was close to finally killing Bossman. She was nearing the end, and the end always brought anxiety.

"We're close," Clay said, glancing at the road ahead. Even though they were near Bossman's campsite, Jade knew Clay wasn't talking about that.

"Yeah," Jade sighed. "We're finally here."

"I'll follow your lead."

Jade nodded.

Bossman was sheathing a machete into his belt loop when they arrived. He smiled when he saw Jade, but it quickly faded when he saw Clay.

"I thought it'd just be us," he said.

"You were mistaken."

Bossman shrugged. "If you want to bring your boytoy along, then so be it."

Jade didn't respond. Now that the moment was finally coming, Jade was finding him less annoying. She would get her revenge soon enough. And that was very comforting.

"The State Capitol is about three and a half miles from here," Bossman said as he gathered his things. "That should give us plenty of time to stake out the area before Cole gets there."

"You think Chase will get there before Cole?" Jade wondered.

"No," Bossman snorted. "He will want to make a spectacle of this. People are questioning his leadership. He will respond publicly."

"That sounds like a lot of people will be in danger," Clay said.

"And you're right about that," Bossman said. "Brains and looks. I see why you like him, my love."

Jade rolled her eyes. "Are you ready?"

Bossman slung his backpack over his shoulders. "Let's go."

They walked the three and a half miles in silence. Jade was surprised. She was convinced that Bossman would spend the time making little remarks about Clay and how he wished they were alone. But he didn't. He remained utterly silent on the matter, which was odd. Jade saw it as a win and kept moving.

It was quiet outside. They barely encountered any people, which Jade expected since they were taking a less-traveled route. They really didn't want people knowing Bossman was nearby. If word got out that he was in the area, people would be less brave in their actions. And they needed everyone to feel fearless.

Despite everything happening around her, Jade remained in shock. She never thought this day would come. She never imagined that the people would become so fed up with the government and its restrictive medical law that they would find the strength and courage to fight back. *Revolt*. It all felt so unbelievable. Yet, Jade still felt grateful for that feeling.

As they approached the Capitol building, Jade was impressed by how many of the surrounding structures still stood and remained intact. Yes, she had heard the rumors like everyone else about how resources were allocated to keep buildings in the state's capitals in good condition, but she didn't expect it to be this extensive. This felt surreal. Despite areas overgrown with foliage, it was hard to tell that much had changed. It reminded Jade of the old days. She felt nostalgic and angry about that.

"There," Bossman said, breaking the hour-and-some-change silence. "We'll hold up in there."

Jade read the signs for Allegan Street and Capitol Avenue before looking in the direction Bossman was pointing. It was a parking garage right across from the Capitol building.

"That's a little close, don't you think?" Clay asked, frowning at the garage.

"The best view in the house," Bossman smirked.

Jade didn't respond. She silently followed as Bossman led them toward the garage's entrance. He took them up a stairwell, and they entered the fifth deck, just below the roof. They walked until they found the perfect vantage point for viewing the building. Jade looked through her binoculars and then frowned. They were on the wrong side of the building. Cole was set to give his speech on the State Capitol's steps. Their current vantage point offered a view of the side of the building.

"We're in the wrong position," Jade said, looking over at Bossman.

"No, we're in the right one," he said casually, looking through his binoculars.

"We don't have a clear view of the steps," Jade shot back.

"We're not here to watch Cole," Bossman reminded her.

"How can you be sure Chase will come this way?" Clay asked instead.

"Trust me," Bossman smiled as he continued to look through his binoculars. "I know my old friend."

Jade sighed and rolled her eyes at his statement. How could he be so sure about this position?

"There's no cover on the side with the main entrance," Bossman lowered his binoculars and looked over at Jade. "City Hall and the State's Office Building are directly across the street. Not to mention, soldiers and DC officers heavily patrol that area. Both who like to see us apprehended or dead."

"Fair enough," Jade sighed. "But why wouldn't Chase go that way?"

"Because he wouldn't want the people to see him coming."

"Shit, it looks like they're expecting something," Clay said, looking through his binoculars.

Jade quickly brought hers back to her eyes. Soldiers were marching out of the main entrance and lining up at the front door, blocking anyone from getting inside. They were on high alert, clearly knowing something was coming.

"I think that's more for Cole's crowd than for Chase," Bossman stated.

"You think they plan on attacking them?" Jade asked, looking over at him. This wasn't part of their plan. There were supposed to be senators aiding them.

"Hold on," Clay said. "There go the senators. Gina, Morris, and Joel are speaking with them."

Clay was right. When Jade looked through her binoculars again, she saw three people in business attire talking with the soldiers. Some of them were nodding as the senators spoke. After a few more minutes, the senators went inside, and the soldiers went back to their posts.

"Ah," Bossman smiled. "The Doc has perfect timing."

Just then, Jade could hear the chants of the approaching crowd. They still sounded distant, but she could clearly hear the words to their chants.

"Out of the red!"

"And into the black!"

"Out of the red!"

"And into the black!"

"Out of the red!"

"And into the black!"

"He has a way with words, doesn't he?" Bossman smirked.

Jade had to agree with Bossman there. Cole's words were definitely chantable. "Into the black" was something that caught on and took on a life of its own. The phrase gave them hope. It gave them a future.

"Out of the red!"

"And into the black!"

"Out of the red!"

"And into the black!"

"Out of the red!"

"And into the black!"

Their words were growing louder now. Jade looked through her binoculars across the street. The soldiers remained still, showing no interest in the approaching crowd. They didn't even turn their heads to watch which way the crowd was coming from. From what Jade could see, Cole and the crowd were heading south on Capitol Avenue, the same way they had come.

"Out of the red!"

"And into the black!"

"Out of the red!"

"And into the black!"

"Out of the red!"

"And into the black!"

It took a few minutes before the sound of their chants became deafening.

"Out of the red!"

"And into the black!"

"Out of the red!"

"And into the black!"

"Out of the red!"

"And into the black!"

They were at the corner of Allegan Street and Capitol Avenue. Instead of turning left onto Allegan like they did, the crowd kept marching down Capitol Avenue, gradually converging on the State Capitol building.

"Out of the red!"

"And into the black!"

Jade was shocked when the crowd came into view.

"Out of the red!"

"And into the black!"

It was more than just the group they had gathered over the past few weeks. It seemed like every citizen of Lansing was out there.

"Out of the red!"

"And into the black!"

It seemed like every citizen of Michigan was out there. The atmosphere was electric.

"This is insane," Clay whispered. Jade could barely hear his words over the noise of the crowd.

"Out of the red!"

"And into the black!"

"The doc has really been working," Bossman said.

"Out of the red!"

"And into the black!"

"No," Jade looked over the massive crowd. "This is the people's frustrations. Cole's just saying all the quiet parts out loud."

"Out of the red!"

"And into the black!"

Finally, she heard Cole's voice cut through the crowd. It was a struggle, but Jade could make out Zara, Yoko, Brice, Jackson, and Cole on the steps of the Capitol building. Cole was standing at the top of the stairs with a bullhorn. The soldiers still hadn't moved.

"Welcome, welcome, welcome," Cole greeted. The crowd immediately fell silent. "I'm so honored that you all decided to join me here today."

The crowd cheered and clapped in response.

"Today we are making history," Cole said. "Today will be talked about for years to come."

Jade watched the crowd. Many people nodded in agreement, while others clapped.

"Today, we're not only telling our government that we've had enough, we're showing them too! We are here to demand change! We demand that they get off their asses and fight for the people!"

The crowd cheered.

"And if they are unable to do that," Cole said calmly. "Then we are here to remove them from their position of power and replace them with someone more suitable!"

More cheers erupted as people clapped and stomped their feet. Jade could've sworn that the parking garage shook from their excitement, but she was positive she was being dramatic.

"Out of the red!"

"And into the black!"

"Out of the red!"

"And into the black!"

"Out of the red!"

"And into the black!"

The crowd started chanting again, and it took some time for Cole to calm them down.

"Today, we are showing this government what new leadership could look like. What new leadership could be!" Cole looked around. "As I've stated once before, I, Dr. Cole Blackwell, would like to take on the role of a new leader... a new President. This country desperately needs a competent and compassionate leader. And with your support, I hope that'll be me."

"We stand with Blackwell!" someone shouted.

"Out of the red!"

"And into the black!"

"Out of the red!"

"And into the black!"

"Out of the red!"

"And into the black!"

"Here we go," Bossman mumbled.

Jade looked over at him. She was about to ask what he meant by that, but then there was an explosion. Jade tried to spot the source. She saw flames and smoke coming from the other side of the Capitol building. People started to scream, but most of them stayed in place. It didn't seem like anyone was hurt in the explosion.

"Stand your ground!" Cole yelled. "We won't be intimidated!"

"Out of the red!"

"And into the black!"

"Out of the red!"

"And into the black!"

"Out of the red!"

"And into the black!"

"Damn, he's impressive," Bossman chuckled. "Let's head out."

"What's happening?" Jade asked as she followed.

"Chase is here," he said, hurrying down the stairs.

"Stand your ground and fight back!" Jade heard Cole yell. The crowd shouted in agreement.

Bossman, Jade, and Clay were walking out of the parking garage when another explosion went off—this time, knocking them back.

~29~

Helena

"Hold!" Helena ordered as she held her knives at the ready. Tatianna and Reagan stood beside her, both prepared to take action when she gave the command. They all watched as the DC guards struggled to break down the barricaded doors of the solitary wing. Sunday ran around helping those who needed wheelchair assistance. Those who didn't need help were arming themselves with some form of weapon. The most common weapon was IV poles, as many were lying around the wing.

The solitary wing was Helena's main focus as they stormed the prison. She told Tatianna and Reagan her destination and encouraged them to come along. Sunday was with her, of course, but Helena needed more than a nine-year-old for backup. Knowing how the prison system worked, Helena first thought the solitary wing would be on the top floor, but she hesitated when they were two floors below.

When she worked in the prison with Razor, Helena swore that the cries she heard from the solitary unit always sounded different from the cries she'd heard in the general population. Of course, Razor used to look at her like she was crazy, but Helena knew the cries were indeed different. That was why she hesitated when they were two floors below the top because she heard the cries. Helena dashed out of the stairwell, and the others followed. No guards were present. They were mainly focused on the breach at the main entrance of the building.

What awaited them instead were battered and broken individuals, mostly women. The scene broke Helena's heart. She already knew the torture and brutality they had endured—it was written all over their faces.

"Take up a weapon and prepare to fight!" Helena told them. Some hesitated to move, and rightfully so, but others quickly obeyed.

Reagan quickly barricaded the doors to the wing. They knew the breach at the main entrance wouldn't keep all the guards distracted. They needed to get ready to fight.

"We're getting you out of here," Helena said as she looked at everyone crowding around her. "So prepare to stand your ground. Prepare to fight for your freedom!"

She wasn't Dr. Cole Blackwell, but Helena tried to imitate him as best as she could. His words had such a strong effect on people that it was almost scary. He could stir them up and make them ready to revolt with just a few words. Helena hoped she could do one-tenth of that for the people in this wing.

Helena looked at the barricaded doors and then back at the people. "They will attempt to break their way through. But we will stand our ground. Once it seems like they're about to breach, I will signal everyone to charge with a raise of my fist. We will overpower them before they can get through. Head toward the staircase on your left at the end of the hall. Kill whoever tries to stop you."

Everyone nodded and mumbled in agreement. They all looked worried but determined. They were prepared to leave. Helena glanced at the five people in wheelchairs. She hoped Razor or someone else would be in the stairwell to help carry them down. Three debtors could wheel themselves, but the other two needed help. Sunday and another debtor were behind them—ready to push when the time came.

"Hold!" Helena commanded as the guards slammed their bodies against the doors again. She couldn't suppress the butterflies in her stomach. She didn't want to lose anyone. For some reason, she was judging the success of this mission by the number of lives lost under her command. Helena shook her head, trying to dispel the negative thoughts. "Hold!"

They all would survive this.

"Hold!"

And finally, the moment arrived. Helena spotted the potential breach and raised her fist in the air. The debtors yelled as they charged forward. Reagan and Tatianna burst through the doors first, followed by debtors swinging IV poles with all their might. The element of surprise was on their side, so the guards responded slowly to the attack. Helena stayed close to Sunday and the other debtor, who was pushing the wheelchairs. She attacked any guard who got too close to them.

"Damnit!" Sunday shouted as she tried to help Helena fight.

"Get to the stairwell!" Helena demanded as she pushed Sunday aside to keep fighting.

"Helena," Sunday tried to object.

"Go!"

A guard attempted to tackle Helena, but she responded by kneeling. The guard paused, looking confused for a moment, then Helena swiftly stabbed him in the gut. She twisted it and then pulled it out. The drawback of this plan was that she had trouble getting up quickly. Another guard was about to knee her when a knife's blade suddenly appeared in his throat. It vanished, and he fell to the ground. Reagan stood in front of her with her hand extended.

"Let's go," she said calmly as she helped Helena to her feet.

"Thanks for that," Helena sighed as she ran. Reagan kept up with her as they headed toward the stairwell.

"Gonna make this hard for me, I see," Reagan smirked.

"Sorry," Helena mumbled. She knew that Clay had likely given Reagan an order to watch her. Although Helena didn't believe it was necessary, she didn't want to make things harder for Reagan.

"I wouldn't expect anything less from a Willer sister."

Tatianna was fighting off a couple of guards while Sunday held the door to the stairwell open. Reagan pushed Helena toward the stairs as she went to help Tatianna. Keeper and some other debtors were carrying the debtors who used wheelchairs down the stairs.

"Time to go," he told Helena.

Helena waited for Tatianna and Reagan before heading down the stairs.

"Everyone is accounted for," Tatianna reported as she placed a hand on Helena's back.

"Good job, boss," Reagan said to Helena as she held onto Helena's elbow. They were guiding Helena safely down the many flights of stairs. Helena held back a laugh at the absurdity of it all. If it eased their minds, then fine.

Sunday glanced back at her with a sigh of relief. Helena smiled at her.

Then they burst through the doors to the main floor amid chaos. People were running everywhere, and there were more prisoners and debtors than guards and officers. Razor was in the middle of the crowd, guiding everyone out, but Helena could tell he was looking for her, too. Their eyes met, and he quickly made his way over to her. His hand slid over her stomach as his lips met hers. They kissed fiercely. Being apart from him was growing harder with each passing day—and her pregnancy.

"All good?" he asked after they broke away from their kiss.

"All good," she said with a smile.

He nodded and looked around. A crowd was gathering around them. "To the Capitol building!"

Everyone responded with a resounding shout.

Razor grabbed Helena's hand as they sprinted out of the Greater Lansing Prison, with a massive crowd behind them. Helena couldn't help but feel a little relieved. They were heading to Jade. They were carrying out phase two of their plan.

All of this was finally coming to an end.

~30~

Jade

Despite having her mask on, Jade struggled to take her next breath. Screams echoed all around her. But these weren't screams of fear; they were screams of anger. Jade could hear the crowd fighting as she tried to get to her feet. *Shit*. There was something wrong with her mask. There seemed to be a crack where her medication sat. The flow of her medication wasn't coming through properly. Luckily, she had some inhalers with her, but she wondered if that would be enough. It had to be.

"What the hell was that?" Jade groaned as her shoulder ached. She winced while trying to massage it.

"Soldiers," Clay guessed as he made his way over to her. Jade noticed he was bleeding from the side of his head. She pulled out her scarf and held it out to him. Clay shook his head as he pulled out a bandana and held it against his wound.

"Will you be ok?" Jade asked.

"I'm not dying yet," he smirked. Jade knew he meant it as a joke, but the phrase affected her. She didn't want to think about Clay dying. She shook her head.

"Chase," Bossman spat as he took off running across the street toward the Capitol building.

Jade didn't understand how, but for a brief moment, she forgot all about him. She didn't notice when he recovered from the explosion, and she certainly didn't care to see if he was okay.

"Shit," Clay said. "Let's go!" He took off running after Bossman.

Jade sighed as she ran after them. She couldn't see Chase (even though she had never seen him before), but she couldn't see much through the crowd. DC officers and soldiers were fighting the protesters. There were also regular people fighting the protesters. It was odd at first, until Jade recognized one of them—a Radical member. Bossman mentioned that Chase had recruited the remaining Radical members to his side. *Great.*

The Radical member recognized Jade and lunged at her.

"You bitch!" the Radical member yelled.

Jade responded by shoving a knife into their chest. She pushed the member aside and kept running behind Clay. He glanced over his shoulder at her.

"I'm fine," she grumbled. She didn't understand why, but everything felt underwhelming to her. The idea of fighting Bossman was quickly approaching. Everything else seemed mediocre in comparison.

The Capitol steps briefly appeared in view. Jade saw Cole, Jackson, Zara, Yoko, and Brice fighting. The soldiers standing in front of the entrance also fought, protecting Cole and the others. It was odd to see a group of soldiers not following the President's orders.

"Jade!" Clay yelled before a fist appeared in her view.

Jade stumbled as the fist hit her chin. She didn't have time to identify her attacker. It was no use. If they were attacking her, then they were the enemy—plain and simple. Jade quickly raised her arm to block her attacker's next blow. She didn't have time to react. It didn't matter. Suddenly, a group of people swarmed her attacker. They knocked him down and started to crowd around him. Some kicked him while others slammed their bats (and other weapons) down on him.

One person helped Jade to her feet. "Go, Jade," they said, nudging her toward the Capitol's steps. "Do what you have to do."

Jade nodded as Clay pulled her along. She was stunned. Did everyone here know her plan? There was a lot of chaos happening, but Bossman was in view, and no one attacked or avoided him. Sure, he was fighting DC officers and soldiers right now, but that didn't mean he was on the debtor's side. And it certainly didn't mean that everything was forgiven. Did Cole let the people in on their plan?

"There," Clay pointed to a side entrance that Bossman was currently entering. She and Clay followed.

They didn't have to go far into the building to catch up with Bossman. Not far from them stood Chase (Jade assumed), with DC officers and soldiers surrounding him.

"Took you long enough," Bossman said as Jade stood beside him.

"Shut it," Jade shot back as she pulled out two knives from her thigh strap.

"Chase," Bossman said, "it's good to see you, old friend."

"I can't say the same, Nick," Chase said. He was barely visible to Jade, considering the numerous officers and soldiers surrounding him. He glanced over at her. "And you must be the infamous Jade."

"And you must be our cowardly leader," Jade said. She subtly noticed senators fleeing out the rear exit. She was determined to distract the President and his men so everyone could get out safely.

Bossman chuckled, and Chase shot him a stern look.

"Don't be so sensitive," Bossman teased. "She's only stating the truth."

"I never thought you'd be on the debtor's side," Chase spat. "What, did you grow a conscience all of a sudden?"

"I don't have a conscience, and I don't give a shit about the debtors," Bossman said coolly. Jade wasn't surprised by this revelation, but she was surprised that he admitted it aloud. "I'm only here for my revenge."

"Revenge?" Chase laughed breathlessly. "You were the one who took things too far!"

"You never had a problem with my tactics before."

"And I thought you were above killing children!" Chase shot back. Bossman remained silent. "Jesus, Nick, how could I ever think you would do something like that?"

"Bullshit," rage-filled Bossman's voice. "As if you didn't murder children with your asinine law. You think children fighting terminal illnesses are miraculously healed?"

"That's different!"

"No, it isn't. And you know it. Just because their blood didn't touch your hands doesn't mean they aren't stained."

"I'm not taking moral advice from someone like you," Chase said, looking around. To Jade, he seemed like a desperate man. "This ends now."

"That, it does, Chase," Bossman lunged at one of Chase's men. And then Chase's men were charging at them.

Jade steeled herself as she faced a soldier head-on. Many hits were exchanged, but many blows also missed. Jade spent most of her time dodging attacks rather than landing them. Her mask was broken, which was clear. She needed to conserve her stamina and avoid her triggers. When she spotted an opening with the soldier she was fighting, she quickly struck the side of their neck and moved on.

This time, the fights couldn't be quick. She didn't have Keeper around to look at her mask, and the environment wasn't ideal for him to work on it. She needed to be smart—draw the attackers to her, dodge more than attack, and when the time was right, land the fatal blow. That was all she could do, and luckily, it was working for Jade.

Bossman drew more attention to himself, causing the soldiers and officers to focus on taking him down. A few officers turned their attention to Clay, but he easily fought them off. Meanwhile, those remaining seemed to have their eyes on Jade. They needed to finish this quickly; they couldn't let Chase escape. Jade was sure he'd run once his men were gone. They had to be smart.

Fine then.

Jade smirked. She would kill these men slowly. First, them. Then, Bossman.

~31~

Razor

The scene around the Capitol building was overwhelming. The sheer display of violence stunned him. Razor had seen his share of violence before, of course, but there was something about this scene that made him feel... different. Razor had a bad feeling, and it wasn't clear why he felt that way. But he knew everything was about to change. After today, nothing would be the same.

The prisoners from the hospital didn't hesitate to join the fight. They quickly mixed into the large crowd. Razor spotted Cole on the steps in front of the Capitol building's main entrance. He was fighting off soldiers who were trying to capture him. Jackson was nearby but distracted by his own fight with some DC officers. Razor began fighting his way toward Cole. Most of the attackers were soldiers and civilians in plain clothes, whom he assumed were Radical members. Razor immediately fought them off.

"Where's Jade?" Helena asked as she frantically scanned the area. Razor had almost forgotten that she was behind him. That's how unnerving this setting felt to him. He glanced around.

Zara and Yoko were positioned to the left at the bottom of the steps, fighting Radical members. Brice was on the right on the lawn, battling some officers. Keeper, Tatianna, and Sunday were just behind Razor, holding back the attackers. Reagan was beside Helena, scanning the area for her brother.

"I'm not sure," Razor grunted as he swung his machete into the gut of an oncoming attacker. "But let's find out."

They all gradually, but surely, made their way to the steps of the Capitol building. Razor stuck his machete into the back of the soldier who was fighting with Cole. He withdrew his blade from the stunned soldier and quickly pushed him aside.

"Have you seen Jade?" Razor immediately asked Cole.

Cole looked around. He seemed a little dazed and confused. "I don't know," he finally said. "It's all been so much. She and Bossman must've made their way inside. I saw a lot of soldiers and officers rush in a while ago."

Razor nodded. He was about to tell the group to go inside when soldiers and officers burst up the stairs from all directions. It was as if they were trying to keep them out of the building. Zara, Yoko, Brice, and Jackson all moved toward them. The fight that followed was intense. Razor was so focused on protecting Helena and Sunday that he left some gaps in his defense. For the first time, it felt like fear had a tight hold on him. The thought of seeing Helena or Sunday die in front of him froze him in terror.

Luckily, Reagan was there to fill the gaps. She was so quick that it took Razor a moment to realize what she was doing. She positioned herself to protect Helena and also cover his weak points. Sunday stood behind Helena, thrusting her knife at anyone who got too close.

"I got you," Reagan said as she cut an officer's leg and then sliced his throat when he dropped to his knees. "Take a moment and get yourself together."

Razor nodded as he tried to focus. What was going on with him? Why did it feel like he was having a heart attack? He needed to breathe. He just needed to breathe. He took a few deep breaths and resumed fighting. He couldn't let Reagan stay in this awkward position. If she focused on protecting Helena and watching him, she was probably leaving herself vulnerable. Razor couldn't let that happen.

It was clear what the problem was: Jade. He needed to see her. Without her in his sights, his anxiety would only grow. He had to make sure she was okay—safe. Once he knew that, he could focus on the mission. All he had to do was keep fighting. He pulled his knife from his holster and fell into autopilot.

Swing the machete.

Thrust the knife.

Swing the machete.

Thrust the knife.

Swing the machete.

Thrust the knife.

Before he realized it, the number of opponents had significantly decreased. Jackson and Reagan were eliminating the last few officers still standing. Razor sighed in relief. Cole looked around, feeling relieved as well. This battle felt very...final. Razor was doing his best to ignore this ominous feeling. The group huddled close together. Razor wrapped one arm around Helena while holding Sunday's hand.

"Finally, a break," Cole sighed. "This has been nonstop since the explosion."

"Yeah," Brice said, looking relieved. "Let's get inside and—."

They all stared at the tip of the blade protruding from Brice's chest in confusion. Brice's mouth hung open, but no sound came out. Zara shouted as blood poured from his chest. Razor's breathing grew shallow. What the hell was going on?

The blade vanished, and Brice fell to his knees. Reagan quickly sliced the officer's throat before he could move. Razor couldn't believe that someone had sneaked up on them. They were all out of it—off their game. This was a fatal mistake on their part. They had been fighting for too long. They were completely worn out.

"Cole, I need ya help," Keeper quickly said as he tried to stop the bleeding from Brice's wound.

To Razor's surprise, Cole stood frozen, staring down at Brice in disbelief. A variety of emotions flickered across his face, and Razor found it difficult to interpret them.

"Cole, now!" Keeper snapped as he lay Brice on his back. More blood began to ooze from Brice, more than Keeper could stop, but he still tried desperately. Tatianna quickly came to his aid, yet the bleeding didn't stop.

Cole still didn't move. It was so unlike him to freeze up. Razor knew the doc could handle pressure. So, what was going on now?

As soon as he was on his back, Brice looked at his injury—fear and confusion on his face. His hands trembled as they pulled away from his bloody chest. He gazed at Cole with a silent plea in his eyes. Whatever kept Cole frozen quickly disappeared. He rushed to Brice's side and tried to help him. But one look at the wound and the amount of blood told them what they already knew.

It was no use. Even Brice seemed to accept it after a few more seconds. Zara cried out loudly again. Razor cleared his throat as he fought to contain his grief.

Brice began moving his hands insistently, as if trying to communicate something to Cole urgently.

"I know. I know, my friend," Cole smiled sadly at Brice. Razor noticed the meekness in his tone. "It was a great honor having you fight by my side. You've carried out the values of our mission beautifully. Rest now. You deserve it."

At these words, Brice took his final breath—a faint smile froze on his face.

The group fell apart then. Razor couldn't help but feel gutted for some reason. They were changing the course of history, but at what cost? And how much were they willing to give?

Razor looked back at the Capitol building. He had to find Jade *quickly*.

~32~

Jade

Frustrated, Jade threw her combat nebulizer on the floor, and it skidded a few feet away. It was now useless. She grabbed an inhaler and took a couple of puffs. Even though she paced herself, Jade's asthma still flared up. *Shit*. The tightness in her chest slowly eased, but Jade knew it wasn't enough.

They had gotten through Chase's men faster than she expected, even with her conscious decision to go slow. Before she knew it, she and Clay were taking out the last officers together. They moved so in sync that Jade wondered how long this had been happening. She looked over at Chase. He was still standing firm in the middle of the main hall. She was pretty impressed. She figured he would've run once his men were dead. But Chase didn't move, not even when Bossman started stalking toward him.

"Shit your pants yet?" Bossman asked as he moved closer to Chase.

Chase scoffed. "As if I'd be afraid of someone like you."

A loud popping sound echoed through the building as Clay pushed Jade to the ground. She looked around, confused. What just happened? Bossman had stopped walking and was clutching his side. He pulled his hand away, and blood was smeared on it.

"Shooting me was your best move," Bossman smirked. "But you should've aimed for the head."

Jade was stunned. Chase shot Bossman. That *was* his best move, but it made Jade furious. She was the only one who could kill him. That was the only way this ended. Clay helped Jade back to her feet.

"That was close," Clay said. "I didn't see that coming."

"Neither did I," Jade said.

Bossman charged at Chase. Chase prepared himself for Bossman's attack. Jade saw a flicker of the gun as Chase lifted it and struck Bossman on the back of the head. Bossman slammed Chase to the ground and knocked the gun out of his hand. Bossman stood over him.

"As if a single bullet could kill me," Bossman said as he stomped on Chase's hand. There was a snap, and Chase yelled out. Bossman grabbed Chase by his shirt. "If I fall, then you're coming too."

Bossman started punching Chase in his face. After a few blows, Bossman lost his grip and yelled as he staggered back. Jade noticed a knife sticking out of Bossman's upper thigh. Chase fell to the floor again as Bossman dropped to one knee.

"I'll make sure you go to hell first!" Chase tackled Bossman, causing both of them to fall. Chase climbed on top of Bossman and started punching him with his good hand. Jade could see that Chase's dominant hand was broken.

As Chase pulled back for his next punch, Bossman headbutted him, leaving Chase stunned. Bossman quickly grabbed Chase by the throat. Chase squirmed for a moment, then started clawing at Bossman's face. Jade tried to step closer for a better look, but Clay stopped her. Bossman then started screaming as Chase crawled away from his grasp. Bossman was holding his left eye with his hand. Chase struggled to get to his feet.

"This is over, Nick," Chase rasped as he staggered to his feet. "This world no longer needs men like you."

Bossman chuckled. "You fight like a frightened little pussy."

"You are done for, you hear me, Nick," Chase tried to shout, but he was still struggling to regain control over his voice. "My purpose for you has been fulfilled."

"Not quite," Bossman smirked. "I got one more mission left in me, boss." He ran unsteadily at Chase. This time, Chase did try to retreat, but even with an injury, Bossman was faster. He tackled Chase back to the ground, but before Bossman landed on top of him, he pulled the knife from his thigh and shoved it into Chase's neck.

Chase's eyes widened at the sudden turn of events. Blood gushed from his jugular. His mouth moved as if he were trying to speak. His good hand weakly pushed against Bossman's chest, fighting until his last breath.

"Goodbye, old friend," Bossman said in a detached tone. "We had a good run."

Jade clenched the knives in her hands and slowly moved out of Bossman's line of sight. Clay positioned himself on the opposite side.

Chase's arm went limp, along with the rest of his body.

Clay charged at Bossman just as he was pulling the knife out of Chase's neck. Bossman swung the knife at Clay, but Clay dodged it. Clay's distraction was exactly what Jade needed. She moved in close to Bossman and jabbed her knife just below his shoulder blade. Bossman quickly elbowed her with his other arm, causing Jade to fall to the floor. Bossman slowly got to his feet, laughing. Jade was quickly back on her feet, pulling another knife out of her holster.

"Smart move," Bossman complimented. He looked back at Clay. "I guess good looks don't make you vapid, aye, boy toy?"

Clay took a few steps back, creating more distance as Jade charged at Bossman again. This time, she went for his legs. Bossman fell over. He tried to shove his knife into Jade's gut, but Clay was there, knocking it out of his hand. Jade drew back to stab Bossman with her own knife, but he caught her wrist before she could bring it down. They struggled for a few seconds. Then Clay had his own knife. Bossman's eyes widened as he twisted himself so Clay's knife could go into his right shoulder. Bossman flung Jade off him, and Clay quickly stood.

"Aiming for the heart, huh?" Bossman said to Clay as he stood. He winced as he pulled the knife from his shoulder. "Sorry, boy toy, I won't be going down that easily."

Again, Jade took advantage of the distraction and rushed in. She slashed at the back of Bossman's knee, the one Chase had stabbed. Bossman yelled as he slashed at Jade. She yelled too. He managed to cut the side of her stomach as she was retreating. She groaned as her hand went to her side.

Clay charged in again. Jade didn't see anything in his hand, and her heart began to race as Bossman was thrusting his knife towards Clay's abdomen. Her chest started to tighten again. She couldn't watch someone else she loved be killed by Bossman again. Then Bossman yelled as the knife slipped out of his hand. Clay quickly grabbed it and shoved it into Bossman's stomach.

"Hiding your weapon," Bossman groaned. "That's such a bitch move."

And to Jade's surprise, Bossman pulled the knife out of his stomach and brought it down on Clay. Jade screamed.

No! Not again! Not again! Not again!

Clay moved, so it mostly went into the top of his shoulder instead of his neck. Jade rushed back into the fight, ignoring that her asthma was about to flare up. Clay pulled out his concealed knife and slashed Bossman's neck. But Bossman was already retreating, so Clay's attack wasn't as fatal.

Jade was slamming into Bossman, and he fell onto the floor with a loud smack. Then she was pinning his arms down with her knees. She was pulling another knife out. Blood was flowing out of her side. Blood was flowing out of Bossman's stomach. A raging red was clouding her vision.

The memory of Raina and Levi's bodies convulsing with blood seeping from their taped mouths, as Bossman's machetes pierced them.

The memory of the light leaving David's eyes as Bossman shot a bullet through his skull.

Every time she blinked, Jade kept reliving those moments again and again. *Red.* All she kept seeing was an overwhelming amount of *red.*

Jade was hyperventilating, her breaths quick and shallow. She needed to calm down and breathe. Tears streamed down her face as she realized she was crying, though she didn't know when it had started.

"Jade," Bossman murmured. "I am sorry... and for what it's worth, I do love you." He coughed. Jade noticed how pale he was starting to look. "In my own twisted way, I loved you as best I could."

Jade's breathing grew faster at this. She didn't want to hear any more of his sick love confessions. She didn't want to hear any more of his half-assed apologies. She wanted him *dead.*

"And I will always love—"

Jade screamed as she plunged her knife into Bossman's chest. His eyes widened in shock. He struggled to breathe. He looked down at the knife in his chest and then back at Jade. A slight smile was briefly on his lips, as if he was proud of what she'd done. Jade glared down at him through tears.

"Fuck your love, *Nick*," she seethed.

Bossman sighed as his head tilted to the side. His breath grew weaker with each passing second. Silence surrounded them—the only sound was Bossman's strained breathing.

Finally, justice. Justice for those who fell victim to this psychopath and the world he created. Justice for those who lost their lives and loved ones because of him. No. Because of *them*. Bossman wasn't the only evil person in this scenario. Chase was just as guilty, if not more. The world was now cleansed of them.

Then, after a few more seconds, with his last breath, Bossman whispered, "Adien."

Clay was instantly at her side and helping her to her feet. She winced as her hand went to the cut on her side. Jade looked down at Bossman's dead body, her knife sticking out of his chest. She was waiting for the wave of relief to wash over her. But Jade didn't feel a thing. Nothing. Instead, she felt empty. Where was the joy? Where was the happiness? She'd gotten her revenge. So, why wasn't she satisfied?

"You did it," Clay said, looking down at Bossman's body. She noticed that the knife was no longer in Clay's shoulder. "You rid the world of him."

"Yeah," Jade said, looking at Bossman's body with a sense of disappointment.

All she could picture was her body lying lifeless with a knife sticking out of her chest. She could've easily been Bossman. Sometimes, she felt like she was him. She has killed so many people during all of this. She didn't feel remorseful, and she hardly ever had nightmares anymore. Jade wasn't any better than Bossman. Would the world be better off without her, too?

"Give it time," Clay said as he gently turned Jade's face to look at him. "After a while, you'll know it was the right thing to do."

"I know it was the right thing to do," Jade sighed. She closed her eyes as she tried to find the words to express her feelings clearly. "It still doesn't feel like...enough." That was the best way she could explain how she was feeling.

Clay nodded. "Your family is alive and growing, Jade. That should be enough to start moving on."

Jade frowned as she processed his words. The growth of her family should be enough. Her anger couldn't comfort her forever. Recently, she hadn't been there for Helena like she should. Jade left everything up to Razor and Sunday, who was nine years old. Once again, she had abandoned her sister for her own selfish reasons. Jade needed to make up for that. Maybe she could make up for all the wrongs she's done by being there for her family.

"You're right, Clay," Jade said. "That's more than enough."

Clay smiled at her.

Jade smiled back, feeling so thankful for him. "Let's get out of here."

"Yeah," Clay looked down for a moment and then back at her. "Jade, I ..."

"I know," she said, cutting him off. "I love you, too."

Clay's smile grew wider as he leaned in to kiss her. Jade returned the kiss, feeling so happy that he was still there. She felt relieved that he had made it through everything. God, she couldn't wait to build a future with him. Clay pulled back, took her hand, and led them toward the nearest exit.

This was the end. They had finally reached this moment.

"I can't wait to find Helena—" Jade couldn't finish her sentence. A rush of heat flooded over her before she and Clay were thrown backward.

Then, the ground began to shake.

~33~

Helena

The tears couldn't stop falling as she watched Brice take his last breath.

It all felt too real for Helena. Panic surged in her chest. Helena looked around frantically. She needed to find Jade. Cole said she might be inside the Capitol building. Helena looked at the others to signal that they needed to get inside, but they were still distraught over Brice's death. Helena glanced over the massive crowd fighting around the building. There was so much violence. There were so many dead bodies.

Why did this feel so wrong?

They fought hard to get here. They suffered so many losses. They've endured so much pain. Yet, they've persevered to build a better future.

So, why did this feel wrong? Why did it seem like they were expected to give more? To sacrifice even more?

Helena was overwhelmed with dread. She couldn't bear any more sacrifices. She glanced at Razor, who was looking back and forth between Brice's body and the building. Helena knew he was thinking about Jade, too. She caught his eye. It looked like he was about to say something when movement around the perimeter drew his attention. It caught hers as well.

A group of soldiers had spread out around the base of the building. Helena squinted to see what they were holding in their hands. As they knelt to place the item on the ground, Razor grabbed Sunday and Helena.

"Bomb!" someone shouted.

Helena hit the ground, and Razor landed on top of her. Then she felt the heat, and it was overwhelming. Tears kept flowing nonstop. Helena felt a tiny hand clutch her arm, and she panicked thinking about Sunday. She couldn't breathe; it felt like she was suffocating. She was gasping for air as she thought about how the heat felt on Sunday—how it felt on *Razor!*

God!

This needed to stop. This *all* needed to stop!

"Razor!" Helena screamed. "Razor!"

Her hands gripped his shoulders, but she couldn't hear him. She didn't feel any response from him.

This needed to stop.

This needed to stop.

This needed to stop!

"Razor!" she kept screaming. He wasn't moving. Why wasn't he moving? Sunday's hand squeezed Helena's arm again, as if trying to soothe her. Tears blurred Helena's vision as anxiety took over her.

Then there was a ringing sound. Helena couldn't hear anything else. What was happening? What was wrong with her?

Finally, Razor shifted, then slowly moved away from her.

"Razor!" she cried.

Specks of debris and dust covered him. He had minor cuts on his face, and some blood was running down the side of his head, but Helena didn't see anything life-threatening. Razor was saying something, but Helena couldn't hear him. His hand nervously went to her stomach, then to her face, and then over the rest of her body. He looked at her with concern as his mouth moved again. Helena shook her head. The ringing in her ears wouldn't stop.

Then Helena felt movement beside her. Razor's attention went there. Helena looked over at Sunday. She was holding her shoulder and wincing in pain. Razor spoke again and looked over Sunday, assessing for further injuries. Sunday looked at Helena and started to talk. Razor shook his head and said something to Sunday. Sunday frowned as she looked at Helena again. After a few more seconds, Razor stood and then he helped Sunday to her feet.

The ringing in Helena's ears was gradually fading. Now, the sounds she heard made her feel as if she were underwater. Everything sounded so muffled and jumbled. Razor now had his hand on her elbow as he tried to help her to her feet. Helena slowly stood. The burning smell in the air made her stomach turn. Instinctively, her hand went there.

The scene was horrific. Cole and Jackson lifted a piece of rubble off Zara, freeing her broken leg. Tatianna and Keeper helped Yoko to her feet as she clutched her torso. Reagan knelt beside someone, trying to stop the bleeding from an injury. Helena kept looking around—taking in the scene. The number of dead and burned bodies was staggering.

Helena couldn't take it anymore. She bent over and vomited forcefully, even though there was barely anything in her stomach. Razor's hand instantly went to her back.

"Helena," his muffled voice said. "Are you ok?"

Helena kept vomiting. She couldn't stop, even when there was nothing left to throw up. She had spent minutes simply heaving and gagging. Tears kept streaming down her face.

Razor kept his mouth close to her ear as he gently stroked her hair. "I'm right here, Helena. It's ok."

Helena shook her head. "Jade," she said once she could speak. "I need Jade." She looked at the Capitol building and cried even harder.

Razor cursed.

The damage to the Capitol building was disturbing. There was a fire burning inside, and the windows had been shattered. Numerous cracks and holes spread across the structure, making it seem like it could collapse at any moment. Could Jade have survived all of that?

"Jade!" Helena cried out again. She tried to move toward the building, but Razor's arm was wrapped tightly around her waist.

She had to get inside to make sure Jade was safe, but then the universe decided to add insult to injury.

The ground shook.

No.

This couldn't be happening. *Not now!* Helena cursed and yelled. They hadn't felt an earthquake in so long; *now, it had to happen?*

The ground shook more violently, and everyone braced themselves. Razor's grip on Helena tightened. Sunday ran over to Helena, and Helena wrapped her arms around her. More parts of the building collapsed. Helena's heart sank. She had to watch agonizingly as the building slowly caved in before her.

After a few moments, the ground finally stabilized. Helena collapsed to the ground, tears streaming down her face.

"Jade, I need you," she whispered, staring at the devastating structure before her.

~34~

Jade

The pain in her gut incapacitated her. Jade had never felt such agony before. Tears streamed down her face, and even that hurt. Jade tried to make sense of what had happened. The explosion caught her off guard, but the earthquake was deadly. She and Clay were knocked back from the blast, and Jade was sure she had some burns.

Still, she pushed herself up. She had to reach Helena. But then the ground and the unstable building shook again. The next thing she knew, Clay was tackling her to the ground, trying to shield her as pieces of the ceiling fell on top of them.

Everything went dark, and then Jade felt something pierce her stomach. Darkness ensued. When she awoke, Jade was overwhelmed by a burning pain in her abdomen. She cried out. Clay groaned. He was still on top of her. Neither of them could move. Jade slowly looked down and saw that a rebar had impaled both her and Clay. They were pinned together.

Jade cried even harder.

No, this was wrong. This was very, very wrong.

She should now be reunited with Helena. They should be celebrating that this was finally over. They should be planning their future. They should be talking about the baby. Joy and happiness should fill the air. But not this.

God, not this.

Jade could feel the blood pouring from her, and there was so much of it.

Not like this. Please, not like this.

Jade couldn't just leave Helena like this. This felt all wrong.

Then her chest tightened. Smoke from the blast hit her lungs, triggering her asthma.

No! This can't be happening. This can't be happening. This can't be happening!

"Jade," Clay managed to say. His hand reached for her cheek as blood covered his mouth.

"No," Jade cried. Reality hit her as she looked back down at the rebar that was impaling them. There was no way either of them was going to get out of this alive.

"Jade, I love you," Clay's voice strained. "I'm so happy I get to leave here with you."

Jade closed her eyes. She tried to take a deep breath, but she cried out in pain again. That was a terrible idea and seemed to worsen the pain.

Not to mention, there wasn't much air reaching her lungs.

"I'm... so... sorry, Clay," she said softly. It was difficult for her to speak. He should be with Reagan. Jade felt overwhelmed with guilt for taking her brother away.

Clay shook his head. "This is where I want to be."

Jade smiled through her tears as she felt Clay's fingers softly wipe them away. He was so kind to her, even in those last moments.

"I love you so much, Clay," she whispered, running her fingers through his hair. The movement of his fingers was slowing down, and Jade knew he was leaving her.

Jade wrapped her arms around him and pressed her face into his neck. Clay's breathing was faint. Jade listened as it grew quieter and quieter, until finally, Clay stopped breathing altogether. Jade cried harder, despite the pain, knowing she would be with him soon and finding comfort in that.

Jade found it increasingly difficult to breathe with each second.

Despite everything, Jade found comfort in knowing she helped create a better environment for her niece or nephew.

This was all for you, she thought. And for your mother and father, too.

I'm sorry, Helena. I did my best to be there for you, but I don't think I can get through this. Stay strong, my sweet sister. You're an amazing woman, and you'll be an incredible mother.

Razor, please continue to protect and watch out for Helena. You were the best brother someone like me could ask for. Thanks for putting up with me and enduring my anger. I don't think anyone has loved me as much as you do. I'm so glad you were in my life.

To everyone else, please continue to support one another and work together to make this world a better place. I love you all.

Jade was feeling cold. Her body was growing weak, and it felt like she could barely breathe. Her arms slowly dropped to her sides.

So, that was it. Death was finally catching up with her.

Jade looked up and saw her mother and father standing before her, smiling. Then Raina and Levi appeared beside them. David was next, followed by Calvin, and then Clay. They all seemed happy to see her. Jade smiled back. Finally, a wave of peace washed over her.

Raina extended her hand. "Come on, Jade," she said with a smile. "Let's go home."

Finally, Jade thought as she took her last breath. *I'm going home.*

~35~

Razor

Failure. *Failure. Failure.* That was all that echoed in Razor's mind as he stared in shock at Jade's lifeless body. *Failure. Failure. Failure.*

They managed to navigate through the Capitol building after the explosion and earthquake. There was a small fire inside that they managed to extinguish. As they explored the building, the group saw Chase's body alongside soldiers and DC officers. Further inside, they spotted Nick's body. It was hard to tell how Razor felt about that. He knew this would probably end with Nick's death, but despite everything, Nick had once been a friend to Razor. So, it was tough to see him gone.

Then, they saw Jade's combat mask. It was practically shattered. Razor's hands trembled as he reached down and picked it up.

"Help me," Reagan demanded urgently to Jackson.

They were near the side exit. The entrance was blocked with debris, and pieces of the ceiling were scattered on the floor. A section of the floor sagged as if it might collapse beneath a large piece of rubble. That's what Reagan needed help with.

Reagan, Jackson, Cole, and Keeper slowly cleared the rubble. Jade's combat nebulizer rattled in Razor's hands.

Then hell broke loose.

Reagan and Helena cried out in pain at the same time. Reagan dropped to her knees as Helena rushed toward the debris site. Cole stopped her before she got too close.

"Let's get them somewhere safer first," Cole told her. Sunday stood nearby, watching nervously.

Razor couldn't move. He was too scared to do so. He looked down at Jade's battered combat nebulizer. Helena's wails filled the air. He couldn't lift his eyes. He simply couldn't. His gaze remained fixed on her mask.

"Jade, no, God, no!" Helena's voice shrieked. "No! Please!"

He didn't want to see it. He didn't. If he didn't look, then it wasn't real. It wasn't true.

"Helena, I'm really sorry," Cole said.

"Reagan, it's going to be ok," Jackson said.

Helena's screams echoed through the building. Razor knew he should go to her side. He should be comforting her, but Razor's body simply refused to move.

"It's ok, Helena," Sunday said weakly.

"We should find something to cover them," Keeper said slowly. He sounded like he was in shock.

"No, please," Helena yelled desperately. "Jade, I need you."

At those words, Razor finally looked up. His legs moved slowly, as if several bricks were tied to them. Helena was lying over Jade's body, while Sunday and Tatianna were on each side, gently rubbing her back. Tatianna kept wiping her eyes, but Sunday didn't bother to wipe her tears. Reagan was kneeling silently by Clay's body, crying quietly. Jackson was beside her, doing his best to comfort her. Yoko and Zara sat on the ground near the main entrance, both too injured to get any closer. Cole and Keeper looked on, stunned. They were all trying to come to terms with these new losses.

As Razor got closer, he finally saw the view he'd been dreading. Jade was dead. She really was dead. Helena had shifted, and he saw what had killed her. There was a hole in the middle of her stomach. He looked over at Clay's body and saw a matching wound.

"A rebar impaled them together," Reagan's voice cracked. She looked up at him. Razor nodded.

This wasn't right. This wasn't real. It had to be a cruel joke. He wasn't supposed to lose her, not like this. If anything, he was supposed to go before them. Razor was meant to die protecting them. The Willer sisters were his heart and soul. They were *his* girls. Both of them were meant to stay in his life. This wasn't right. He couldn't lose someone he loved so much like this.

"That's the problem, Razor," he recalled Jade saying to him. *"You love me so much that it might be the death of you."*

Shit. She was right.

Razor dropped to the ground. Cole and Keeper managed to catch him before he hit the floor too hard. Razor felt like he was dying. When did he stop breathing? He was gasping for air, but it seemed like it refused to reach his lungs. Where was the air? He needed it!

Why didn't he listen more carefully to her warning?

"You love me so much that it might be the death of you."

He was distracted by how beautiful she looked at that moment. He was mesmerized by how her brown eyes sparkled through her tears. He was captivated by how hurt she seemed when she thought he wouldn't choose her, too. Everything about that day and that moment made him ignore the warning she was trying to give him.

"You love me so much that it might be the death of you."

"Jade," he cried out, gasping for breath. He looked into her vacant eyes. Those beautiful brown eyes weren't sparkling anymore. She was gone. She really was gone.

"Jade!" Razor cried out more urgently. Razor had never heard his voice sound like this before. It was so broken—so shattered.

Helena glanced at him and quickly threw herself into his arms. Razor, without thinking, wrapped his arms around her.

"Razor, I'm so sorry," she cried.

"This can't be real," he whispered. "She can't be gone."

Razor didn't know how long he and Helena had cried in each other's arms. He didn't know what the others were doing during that time. He was too lost in his grief to notice anything else. But finally, Cole knelt beside him and placed his hand on his shoulder.

"My friend," Cole said softly. It seemed like he had been crying too. "It's time to move them."

Razor nodded.

Keeper approached with a long piece of fabric in his arms. He stopped in front of Razor and Helena. "I'm going to cover them before we move them."

Razor noticed it was a torn piece of the state flag. He looked at Jade one last time. God, he was going to miss her dearly. He would miss the sound of her voice. He would miss her constant questioning. He would miss her rage. He would miss their bickering and fighting. He would miss her relentless worrying over others. He would miss being the shoulder she'd cry on. He would miss feeling her wrapped in his arms. He would miss seeing what she would become in this new world. He was going to miss it all.

As the fabric gradually covered Jade's lifeless body, Razor couldn't help but wonder if it was all worth it.

~*Six Years Later*~

Razor

The anger behind the brown eyes watching him made Razor sigh. What did he do wrong now? Lately, it felt like he couldn't do anything right. Even the way he breathed seemed to be wrong.

"Would you stop glaring at me, Jade?" Razor sighed as he sheathed the knife.

"I don't understand why I can't have it," Jade whined as she kept glaring at him.

"Because you're too young."

"Am not!" Jade stomped her little feet.

Razor smirked as he looked down at his daughter. She wore her signature glare, which he loved. Her hair was curly and unruly. Her cocoa skin looked smooth and nearly flawless. There was a scar on the corner of her chin, a result of an accident from climbing a tree a few months ago. Helena had told her how much her aunt Jade used to love climbing trees, and eager to be just like her, their daughter decided to try it herself. Now, she wore the scar like a badge of honor.

"Do you want your mother to kill me?" Razor asked.

Jade giggled. "She won't kill you, Daddy. She loves you too much."

"I'm glad you're so confident about that."

"Can I please just look at it?" Jade pouted. Her small lips were fully pushed out. She was really giving it her all. Why did she have to look like her mother right now?

Razor sighed in defeat as he knelt beside her. They were in their backyard. Jade was outside playing when Razor came to check on her. She was sitting under a tree (the one she fell from), looking at something. To his surprise, she was staring at her aunt Jade's old knife. Razor quickly took it from her, marking the start of the whole ordeal.

"Just look," Razor warned as he unsheathed the knife.

Jade smiled as she stared at it, her brown eyes sparkling with awe. Razor couldn't help but smile; he loved those eyes and was so afraid he might never see them again.

"Sissy said this will be mine someday," Jade whispered.

"Did she now?" Razor asked, raising an eyebrow.

Jade nodded, still fascinated by the knife. Her small hand hovered just above it—barely not touching. Razor smiled. His little girl had a talent for trying to bend the rules.

"I suppose she's the one who showed you where it was, too," he would talk with Sunday when she returned from visiting Tatianna and Keeper.

"Don't be mad at sissy, Daddy," Jade said. "I begged her to tell me more about Auntie."

Razor sighed as he sat on the ground and pulled Jade onto his lap. He handed her the knife. "Careful," he warned. "Don't cut yourself."

"I won't," Jade whispered while gripping the handle.

Razor kissed her forehead. Yet another Willer female he couldn't say no to. "What do you want to know?"

"What was she like?"

Jade often asked about her Auntie. Many people shared stories about her. Buildings and streets were named in her honor. Plaques in parks and museums celebrated her legacy. Jade is now even mentioned in history books as a revolutionary leader. With Cole now serving as President, he made sure that everyone involved in overthrowing the old government was recognized in some way.

Cole was proving to be a great President. The medical law was quickly abolished, and he began working hard to create a government and system that the people could trust. Jackson and Yoko moved with Cole to D.C.. Reagan and Zara traveled from state to state, overseeing the implementation of new policies and laws for Cole. Tatianna and Keeper stayed in Michigan with him, Helena, and Sunday. Tatianna had just given birth to a baby boy.

Things were beginning to feel normal once more. There hadn't been any unusual natural disasters since Jade died. Neighborhoods and cities had been rebuilt. Law and order had been restored. Money was flowing again. Job markets had been revived. Hospitals were functioning properly. The rebuilding of civilization was taking place all around the world. Jade had played a part in that.

"She was amazing," Razor said, looking out into the yard. "She was fierce, loving, courageous, stubborn, curious, and just."

Razor paused as his heart ached. There hadn't been a day that he hadn't missed her. He knew Helena felt the same. Some nights, he'd hear her crying for her sister, and Razor would cry along with her. The pain of not having her here would never fade; Razor had just learned to live with it.

"She was determined to create a better and safer world for you," Razor said as he kissed the top of his daughter's head.

"For me?" Jade looked up with wonder in her eyes.

"For you," Razor kissed his daughter again. "She loved you so much she sacrificed her life for you."

Jade frowned as she looked back down at the knife. "I wish she could have stayed."

"Me too," Razor looked at the knife in Jade's hand. "I wish she could've stayed too."

"Dad!" Sunday called out as she came out of the house. "Mom said it's time for dinner."

Razor took the knife from Jade, and they both stood up. He grabbed Jade's hand while holding the knife in his other hand. "Look what I found."

Sunday grimaced. "I'm sorry, Dad. But you know how Jade gets."

Razor chuckled as he sheathed the knife. "I do," he said, pulling her into a hug. He couldn't believe she was 15 now. "Welcome home. How was babysitting?"

"Oh my God, baby Parker is so cute!" she squealed. "His chubby cheeks are to die for."

"I want to see baby Parker!" Jade whined.

"He's in the house with Auntie Tati and Uncle Keeper," Sunday extended her hand to Jade. Jade immediately grasped her sister's hand, and they both headed to the house.

Razor watched them and smiled. He looked down at the knife in his hands. It was one of the knives Jade kept in her holster—and her favorite.

She had collected many of them during their time together, but this one was found while they were scavenging one day. It was just a regular combat knife, but Jade insisted it called to her. Razor had looked at it, and it seemed good enough. It was a straight-edged knife with six pieces of brown leather wrapped around the handle.

Jade used it often, and it had helped her out of some tight spots. Razor wasn't sure why, but he kept that knife as a keepsake. He maintained it—sharpening it and preventing rust. When their daughter turned one, the thought of giving it to her consumed his mind. Jade would have wanted her niece to have it. Once she was old enough, she would.

Helena walked out of the house toward him, a smile on her lips. Her signature mint green hair was freshly bleached and dyed by Tatianna and Sunday. Razor smiled as she approached him. God, how he loved her. After all these years, his love for Helena had never faded.

"Are you coming inside?" she asked, wrapping her arms around his neck.

"Yeah," he wrapped his arms around her waist and kissed her lips. "I was just thinking."

"About?" Helena raised an eyebrow.

"Everything we've been through," he could see Sunday, Jade, Tatianna, Keeper, and baby Parker through the kitchen window. They were sitting at the kitchen table, laughing and talking. "And if it was all worth it."

Helena sighed as she rested her head on his chest. "And was it?"

Razor buried his face in her hair, inhaling her scent—that familiar smell he always loved. The smell reminded him so much of Jade. Razor sighed with relief as he looked back at the kitchen window. "It definitely was."

The End

ACKNOWLEDGMENTS

Saying it's unreal to be here is an understatement. I can't believe I made it to the end of this series. What an incredible journey it has been! The *Surviving Red Series* has officially wrapped up, and I'm at a loss for words. I've shed tears while writing this series. These characters have been close to me since 2016. Saying goodbye to them feels like saying goodbye to old friends. They will always be in my heart, and I hope they will always be in yours.

Oddly enough, the creation of this series began as an open letter expressing my frustrations with the United States' medical system. While I was writing and editing the last book in this series, which exposed an already flawed system, more of it was being dismantled by the current regime. As a result, even more vulnerable people are left without their basic needs and rights. I have voiced my anger and frustrations through Dr. Cole Blackwell's speeches. I hope his words bring you comfort and encouragement.

I want to dedicate this series to everyone who has faced the challenges of our healthcare system. To the black girls who love everything dystopian, this series is for you. And to anyone who appreciates literature that reflects societal issues, this series is for you.

As always, I want to thank you, the reader, for taking the time to explore this world I've created. I look forward to hearing your thoughts on this series.

I want to thank everyone who helped me put together this book, including the cover artist, beta readers, proofreaders, editors, my husband, Fred, family, friends, and others. Your support has meant a lot to me.

Last but certainly not least, I want to thank God for guiding me on this writing journey. I appreciate you for pushing me whenever I started to become complacent.

Thank you for surviving the red and earning your way into the black.

Until the next time,

Jana` Chantel

ABOUT THE AUTHOR

Jana` Chantel is a writer from Detroit, MI. She holds a BA in Creative Writing from Grand Valley State University. Her works include: *Into My Mind*, a collection of personal essays, and her debut dystopian series, *Surviving Red, Razor & Helena: A Surviving Red Prequel*, and *Fighting Red*. When she isn't writing, Jana` works on a creative project with her husband at their company, About Right Media Group. *Into the Black* is the final book in the *Surviving Red series*.

www.janachantel.com

Substack:@janachantel

Facebook.com/authorjanachantel

Tik Tok & Instagram: @janachantel_theauthor